Mr. January
Mercer's War Series
Book 1

By

Jordan Dane

Mr. January

Dedication

To Debbie & Denise

Sisters make the best friends

Dear Readers,

I've been blessed with very dear girlfriends in my lifetime. (You know who you are.) They have gotten me through hard times and hilarious times. The character of Zoey Meager in this book risks everything for her bestie Kaity—even her life. If any of my dearest friends need someone to drive their white Ford Bronco, toss me the keys. I'm in. This book is for the sisterhood of the traveling wine bottle.

I love a brooding angsty man and Mr. January pushes all my buttons. He's got a thirst for unconventional justice and has recruited an eccentric team to carry out his missions and back his play. A mysterious woman benefactor covers his sweet backside. This is book #1 in a new series for me – Mercer's War. I hope you enjoy the action-packed tale of Zoey Meager and Mr. January.

One of the biggest hurdles for an author is 'visibility' online. A rating or review on Amazon, Barnes & Noble, and Goodreads is invaluable, and very much appreciated. Honest reviews and ratings boost a book's placement in searches and that increases sales and discoverability. Please consider rating/reviewing this book and thank you for your support.

Jordan Dane

Chapter 1

Denver, Colorado
Midnight

"My friend could be inside. *Please!* You can't just let her die."

The heat of the flames seared her body, but Zoey Meager didn't care. She seethed against the two firemen holding her back. When she heard another explosion from the three-story warehouse, she raised an arm to cover her face and cringed as more windows blew out. Glass pummeled the ground like molten rain and black smoke mixed with red embers to spiral into the night sky.

"Let me go in. I'll take my chances." She struggled against the two burly firemen.

"No one goes inside." A familiar voice cut through the din.

Larger than life and dressed in turnout gear, Sam

Riggs blocked her path and placed a gloved hand on her shoulder. She knew the fireman from the hospital where she worked as a nurse.

"Police say we have a potential hostage situation, Zoey," he said. "It's not safe for my men, or anyone. I'm sorry. We have to stand down until we get the 'all clear' from the police."

When she saw the pained look on his face, she stopped fighting. He hated this as much as she did. The Denver SWAT team—dressed in full tactical gear in their navy BDUs—had established a perimeter. Even if she found the guts to run into a burning building, she didn't know if she could evade a highly trained SWAT unit.

She stared into the raging fire and hopelessness consumed her. Tears stung her eyes and drained down her cheeks. *Kaity.* She'd been sure this time. Now she prayed she'd been wrong with all her heart as the fire destroyed everything.

"I'm sorry, Zoey." Riggs gripped her shoulder before he let her go. "Real sorry."

She knew Riggs and his men resented being sidelined when lives were at stake. If a gunman held hostages inside, she understood why police had taken control of the scene.

Zoey quit fighting the two men who braced her arms until they released her. She sank into the shadows, feeling useless, and took a deep breath. She slumped against the hood of a police cruiser with its spiraling light bar and stared up at the beams of red and blue cutting through the darkness, with her mind reeling.

Firefighters stood to her right. They could only watch as flames ravaged the abandoned warehouse. Each face had a grim expression colored by regret. She understood the anger of being forced to accept defeat before the fight had begun.

Dense smoke tainted the acrid air and an intense red glow painted the pitch-black sky. Ambulances and police vehicles continued to arrive—Code 3—with bystanders and news crews gathering in the distance. The scene looked and sounded chaotic, but nothing distracted her from imagining the horror her friend Kaity could be facing inside.

She pulled out her cell phone and raised it to her ear, listening to the last message she'd received from Kaity—a message she couldn't delete. She hadn't played it for anyone. *Oh, Kaity, I'm so sorry.* Zoey felt a lump in her throat and shut her eyes to pray, hoping God would hear her. When she opened her eyes again, she saw movement inside the warehouse.

Someone lurked in the shadows.

"Kaity?" she whispered.

This time she wouldn't let anyone stop her.

***

Minutes later

Zoey crept along a back wall and scaled a fence to drop to the other side. Two large loading bays were dead ahead. She crouched in the dark, looking for the best way in when she heard the sound of a faint whimper. Zoey turned toward the noise.

What the hell?

A massive black dog sat on its haunches not five yards from her. She braced for an attack, but the dog didn't appear interested in her. It looked more like a lumbering bear with wise and soulful eyes, as if it weren't an animal at all. It stared into the warehouse with its ears perked and eyes alert. Its feet were restless as if it would run, but it stayed put, rooted in place.

"What's up, big guy?"

The dog didn't waver. Even if she'd been a T-bone, the fierce-looking animal wouldn't have budged. But before she gave the dog a second thought, Zoey saw a police tactical team emerge from the shadows. If she didn't move fast, the cops would block her only way into the building.

"Sorry, boy. You're on your own," she whispered.

Sticking to the shadows, she raced for the delivery ramp and ducked inside the building. Everything turned black. She couldn't see her hand in front of her face until her eyes adjusted. Her breaths became shallow out of necessity. Too much smoke made it impossible to take a full breath.

With her hands out in front of her, she found a perimeter wall and felt her way to a door and into a larger section of the warehouse. Her stinging eyes desperately searched for Kaity.

Please, God. Help me find her.

As she peered through the murky air, she tore off a sleeve of her T-shirt and searched for water. From her work at the hospital, she knew that smoke inhalation was the leading cause of death from fires. When she found a utility sink and a faucet, she doused her cotton sleeve in water and pulled it over her head to cover her nose and mouth.

She'd have only minutes to rush through the building. It had to be enough. But when the smoke became too thick, Zoey knew what to do. She dropped to her knees and crawled. Every second turned into an eternity. The damp cloth across her face steamed in the intense heat as she called out to Kaity. It didn't take her long to realize she had to conserve energy.

Within minutes the fire would surround her—and she'd run out of time.

Move it. Now!

Everywhere she searched, the rooms glowed in blood red amidst choking black smoke. Flames belched through doorways and consumed everything in sight. The scorching heat burned her skin through her clothes. Even the hair on her arms singed when she got too close to the fire and Zoey smelled her hair smoldering.

She forced her mind to focus on her search, despite her growing fear, but another danger posed a problem.

Not knowing what had caught fire, the closed-in structure made it a real possibility that super heated gases, carbon monoxide or hydrogen cyanide might build inside the dilapidated warehouse. She'd learned from firemen when she treated victims that a rolling structure fire could annihilate an older building in a hurry, but toxic fumes could kill anyone long before the fire got to them. Would she even know the gas was killing her?

Panic ate at her resolve, but she kept going.

Zoey had searched most of the first floor without a sign of Kaity or anyone else. A couple of back rooms were all that remained. With two floors above her, she had to cover ground without wasting time. Until she got upstairs, she had no idea how bad the fire would be higher up.

She pushed herself farther down the hall, making her way to every door, but a loud sound caught her off guard.

"What the—?" She stopped crawling. "Kaity?"

Zoey heard a bang. It jarred her and made her jump. Loud splintering cracks sounded like gunfire, but with the noise reverberating off brick in the cavernous space, she couldn't tell which way it came from.

"Kaity!" she cried.

As the heat intensified, she crawled faster and deeper into the storehouse, gagging and coughing. She almost turned back, but she decided to scramble toward the last open door. Whoever had set the blaze must've done it nearby. The flames were more concentrated toward the rear of the first level.

When she detected a vaguely familiar chemical odor in the air, she realized she'd smelled it before, but she couldn't place it. The fire must've been started using an accelerant, but if the rumor of hostages being held was true, who would've set the fire? *Why?*

A man ran from the last room. He didn't see her on the floor and tripped over her. His boots smacked hard against her ribs. The blow shocked her and knocked the wind from her lungs. When she took a tumble, her skin scraped rough brick and pain racked her body.

Zoey smelled blood when the man toppled over her. The coppery tainted scent came off him.

"Stop. Who are you? Where's Kaity?" she screamed. Her vision blurred and her head spun.

Don't black out. You lose it now and you're dead.

Dressed in black, the intruder loomed over her like a nightmare, but she didn't hesitate. Zoey grabbed his jacket in her fist and tightened her grip. When he winced, she noticed the blood draining down his sleeve. He'd been stabbed or shot. Her eyes trailed down to the back of his hand where she saw a tattoo wrapped around his wrist—the head of a snake.

"Police...they're surrounding the building. You can't get away with this." She refused to give up.

"Let go. Now." His deep gritty voice prickled her skin and her throat clenched tight at the sheer size of the man.

He ignored her and struggled to his feet, but Zoey refused to let go. He was the only clue she had for what happened. With her other hand, she grappled for his leg and yanked. He hit the floor with a miserable groan. She crawled toward him and climbed onto his back, but he flipped her to the ground and pinned her.

"You know where she is. I know you do." Zoey bucked under his weight until she saw stars. She pummeled him with her fists, but her muscles grew weaker the longer she struggled. In seconds, she lost feeling in her arms and legs.

Sheer panic mixed with a deathlike indifference as she thrashed against him. In the thickening smoke, she couldn't breathe and her lungs burned from the strain. He loomed over her as her world faded into darkness, marred only by spinning points of light as her final trace of consciousness left her.

Zoey was dying—and she knew it.

Chapter 2

St. Joseph's Hospital
Denver, Colorado
After 2:00 a.m.

"Can you tell me your name?" A woman's voice. "Open your eyes for me?"

Zoey forced her eyes open and winced with the pain. Every inch of her body ached. A blurred image hovered over her. Slowly colors bled into clarity and a face took shape.

A woman's face.

"There you are." She wore blue scrubs and she smiled. "Stay with me. You're at St. Joseph's Hospital. Can you tell me your name?"

"Z-Zoey...M-Meager." She grimaced. "St. Joseph's? How—?"

She could've told the woman she worked as a nurse at another hospital—and maybe earned an insider advantage—but decided against being a team player.

"Do you remember the fire?" the nurse asked.

Fire? Yes, I remember.

She had to focus and keep her mind clear. She refused to be sick, but she had to know what could happen to her. Smoke inhalation symptoms could manifest up to thirty-six hours later. Pulmonary edema was a real possibility. The hospital would want her to stay under observation for up to forty-eight hours.

Kaity's sweet face leached from the darkness of her memory. Was she dead?

No, this can't be happening. How did I get here? What happened to the man in the warehouse—the one who'd tried to kill me?

"Yes. I remember the fire. Who brought me here?" It hurt to speak, but she tried not to show the pain.

"Paramedics treated you at the scene and brought you here. You were unconscious."

"What happened to the man?"

"What man?"

"The guy who—?" Zoey didn't finish. She didn't have time for twenty-questions.

She looked down at her body to assess what the doctors had done.

Zoey saw an intravenous fluids line taped to the back of her hand. A cardiac monitoring machine beeped quietly in the background and she'd been given supplemental oxygen through a nasal cannula, a plastic tube plugged into her nose and fitted around her ears, to prevent hypoxia.

Her mind raced with a checklist of the treatment she had probably been given for smoke inhalation—as well as the dangers she would face.

Would their initial treatment be enough?

They had probably given her antibiotics and corticosteroids to suppress inflammation and reduce any edema if she'd been exposed to heated gases, carbon monoxide or hydrogen cyanide. She still had the real possibility of a secondary infection since smoke inhalation made the airways more susceptible to bacteria.

It could take two to three days for that to show.

No. I can't lie here. I have to know what happened to Kaity.

"Where's my cell phone...my personal stuff?"

"Your clothes are hanging in that closet." The nurse pointed to a door behind her. "And your cell phone and other things are in this drawer."

"Good, thanks."

"The doctor will be here shortly. I'm at the nurses' station. If you need anything, hit the button." The woman raised the call button and clipped it closer to her hand.

Zoey smiled and said, "I'll be here."

She lied.

***

Denver, Colorado
3:20 a.m.

Homicide Detective Estefan Cruz walked through the smoldering carcass of the destroyed warehouse with a thick dank odor filling his nostrils. Water damage fused with the fire's destruction, raising a smothering stench. Between arson investigations and homicide, Cruz had to toss more than a few suits over his career. The odor of human decomp was especially bad. It's why he only bought cheap suits, even though his fashion taste ran higher.

In the darkness he hit the switch to his Kel-light.

The beam stretched into the void and captured fine particles of dust in its wake—a reminder of why the air smelled stale and thick. The scorched shell had turned into a macabre landscape in black and gray. Past the entrance where he had come, an eerie hum drifted through the gutted cavern, leading him like a beacon.

Cruz heard voices ahead, the words garbled by the distance and the steady whir coming from a power generator. With the electricity gone, the portable generator would allow CSI techs to work by floodlights to bag and tag evidence and take digital photographs.

Cruz spotted Detective Kyle Dravin standing near an open door. He stared down into what looked like a storage room.

"What do we have?" he asked the younger man.

"Three women. Bound and gagged. All dead. Coroner thinks they died of smoke inhalation, but he won't confirm that until the autopsies."

Cruz shoved by Dravin and stepped into the room, steeling his spine for what he would see. The bodies of three women were slumped in a corner. Ligature marks, from barbed wire that bound their hands and feet, had cut deep into their bloated skin.

Their faces were contorted. Smoke had darkened their noses and the skin of their faces with soot, but the heat had swollen their eyes, cheeks and lips to make them unrecognizable.

Cruz lived with many ghosts in his years as a homicide cop. He had no doubt these poor young women would haunt his dreams.

"Barbed wire. That's different," he said to Dravin. "If this has anything to do with trafficking, see if you can find any other cases like this. Run your query against ViCAP."

The FBI's national crime database would allow Dravin to reach beyond their jurisdiction.

"Will do. Paramedics also treated one young woman and took her to St. Joseph's. SWAT located her behind the loading bays, unconscious. Hospital called to say her name is Zoey Meager. She's awake. You want me to question her?"

"No. You finish up here. I'll do it." Cruz headed for the door, but stopped. "She was treated for smoke inhalation by EMTs?"

"Yeah." Dravin consulted his notes. "Why?"

"If Zoey Meager had to be treated for smoke inhalation, that means she was inside. How did she get out?"

Dravin shrugged.

"Sounds like an excellent question for Ms. Meager. That's why they pay you the big bucks."

"Smart ass." Cruz left the storage room and headed to where he'd seen Jack Appleton, arson investigator.

The older man had staked a spot near the storage room, collecting evidence into plastic tubs.

"What've you got, Jack? Talk to me."

"I'm seeing signs of an accelerant. Arsonists believe fire destroys evidence of their tampering, but not if a good investigator knows what to look for."

"Thank the good Lord we have you, Jack."

"Pass that on to my boss." The seasoned arson investigator pointed to a spot against the wall. "You see the pattern here? Arsonists forget that only the vapor burns, not the liquid part of the fuel. For material saturated with an accelerant, the wetness prevents the materials from burning. That leaves behind evidence for us to connect the dots. If we match the cloth to something that's in the possession of a suspect, we've got a link to the crime scene. It's worth a shot."

"What do you have so far?" Cruz asked.

"I've been examining patterns of burn, the

structure of the building itself, the ventilation factors, and what fuel loadings were available. Most old warehouses are veritable powder kegs, but we found pour patterns to indicate this is where someone started the fire."

"Is that blood on the cement?" The detective knelt down near a brown stain on the floor. "I'm sure your eagle eye took trace on this?"

"You know it." The man grinned. "I'm still collecting evidence. Looks like a struggle happened here, but I can't be sure when it may have happened. As for the fire, I'm enclosing what I find in air-tight containers to prevent cross contamination and keep the integrity of the accelerant intact, but it looks like arson, deliberately set."

Cruz shook his head. He had no doubt that whoever set the fire had intended to kill any witnesses. The fire had been started near the only ventilation they had. Their bodies hadn't burned. He hoped they could ID the women easier, but they had died in abject fear, killed by the gases and smoke billowing into their death chamber.

The women in the locked storage unit had been nothing more than collateral damage, but one young woman had escaped their fate—Zoey Meager. He reached for his phone to call Central.

"Get me everything you have on Zoey Meager. I'm heading to St. Joseph's now."

He wanted to believe the only witness to the fire would be as innocent as the women who had died in the blaze, but he knew better than to assume. In his career with DPD, he'd seen the cruelty of the most depraved human beings.

Zoey Meager could've escaped her abductors—or she could be a heartless killer.

Chapter 3

Warehouse District

Denver, Colorado

Dawn

He peered over his shoulder one last time before he headed down the shadowy alley. He couldn't afford to be careless. No cars. No foot traffic. He melded back into the darkness and eyed the windows above where he stood. When no one stared down from the condemned warehouse across the street, he drew a sigh of relief.

No one had seen or followed him home. He'd made sure.

He turned and headed deeper into the alley. It took everything he had to keep his boots moving, one foot in front of the other. His wounded arm had grown numb and his fingers tingled. His head spun from the blood loss and he could barely keep his eyes open.

It had been two days since he'd last slept.

Karl had been smart to leave. He didn't blame him.

Too many cops had surrounded the warehouse. He almost didn't get away. He'd messed up and gotten shot because he'd taken a chance by going into the burning building. But if the shooter had seen his face, he would have finished the job and put a bullet in his head.

Damned woman. Why the hell had she risked her life?

If he hadn't rushed into the flames for another reason, she would've died. He'd stayed long enough to haul her outside and made sure someone found her. She could've blown everything if the cops had hauled his ass to jail.

Need sleep. Get patched up.

Wincing, he reached up with his good arm to pull down the fire escape and lumbered up the metal stairs. On the third floor, he yanked on a window and slid it open. He straddled the ledge and lingered to let his senses work.

Everything looked the same. He sniffed the air

for smells only he would know and he listened to the utter stillness, the emptiness of the place. After he was sure no one lurked in the dark, he crawled inside and headed for the utility sink.

A broken mirror hung in pieces on the brick wall. Smeared with soot, his blackened face stared back, cut into slivers like a nightmarish kaleidoscope. He reeked of smoke, sweat and blood. He grimaced with pain as he shrugged out of his shirt, careful not to start the bleeding again, and tossed his dirty clothes in a heap at his feet.

He stood naked at the sink and washed off. Every move took effort. Panting, he put on fresh clothes—a pair of faded jeans and a black T-shirt—before he sacrificed a white tee to dress his wound. The bullet had gone straight through. No bones broken. He'd been lucky. He only hoped his good fortune meant no infection. The blood loss made him dizzy and he already felt feverish, but before he slept, he had to fuel the furnace of his body.

Stacked on a windowsill, he had bottles of water and a few energy bars stashed in a plastic container. He grabbed one of each and forced himself to eat and drink as he watched a rat scurrying into the shadows across the room.

Live and let live. The rat had staked a claim first.

After he ate and drank, he cleaned his bloody mess and set out stuff for when he saw Karl. He eyed the mattress on the cement floor and collapsed into it. His eyelids grew heavy as he stared into the rafters and metal ductwork. He drifted into a fitful sleep until he heard the sounds of footfalls on the fire escape stairs.

On gut instinct he reached for the SIG Sauer P226 that he kept stashed by his bed and racked the slide to chamber a round. He took aim toward the open window. A familiar shadow eclipsed the steel gray of the early morning and clamored inside.

"It's about time, Karl." He lowered his gun and put it away.

The black Tibetan Mastiff padded toward him—ignoring the food and water he'd set out—and crawled into bed with him. Karl burrowed his head into his good shoulder and whimpered, licking his hand.

He heaved a sigh and shut his eyes.

"Yeah, I missed you, too. Don't hog the bed."

***

St. Joseph's Hospital

7:00 a.m.

Detective Estefan Cruz parked outside the ER and entered St. Joseph's Hospital through a set of sliding doors. He stepped up to the ER check-in and caught the eye of the receptionist.

"I'm here to see Zoey Meager. She was brought in last night. What room is she in?"

A petite blond in a nurse's uniform typed the name onto a keyboard and stared at the monitor until she found the room.

"She's in 302." The nurse pointed. "Down this hall, you'll find an elevator. She'll be on the third floor, follow the signs by room number. You can't miss it."

"Thanks." The detective turned to leave.

"No problem."

Cruz cringed and stopped in his tracks. *No problem?* He hated those two words. Whatever happened to 'my pleasure' or 'you're welcome?' He heaved a sigh and carried on. When he got to the third floor and room 302, he found it empty. He looked in the bathroom and the closet for personal belongings, but the room showed no indication it was occupied.

He accosted the first nurse he saw in the corridor.

"Where's Zoey Meager, the woman who's supposed to be in 302?" he asked. "Has she checked out?"

Hospital staff had already told DPD she would be under observation for forty-eight hours. His hinky meter buzzed in his head. Something didn't smell right.

"Let me see."

He followed the nurse to her station on the floor and waited until she looked up Meager's record.

"I don't show her being checked out. Let me confirm that with her doctor. It'll only take a minute."

While the nurse made the call, Cruz's phone rang. The display showed the name. It was Detective Kyle Dravin.

"Cruz."

"I'm still at the scene of the fire. I was about to finish up until I saw a familiar face in the crowd of looky-loos."

"I'm not in the mood for a guessing game, Dravin. Spit it out."

"Zoey Meager. She turned up, out of the blue. I'm holding her in a squad car. What do you want me to do?"

"Detain her for questioning. Take her to Central and wait for me."

"Will do."

Cruz ended the call with his mind stewing on Zoey Meager. Why had she run from the hospital and returned to the scene? Reasons flooded his head—none of them good.

***

Denver Police Department
Central Station
8:10 a.m.

Zoey had seen enough cop shows on TV to know detectives left suspects 'in the box' to observe them from a two-way mirror. She fidgeted in her seat and tried to act normal—avoiding a nervous glance at the observation window—but what the hell did 'normal' mean any more? When she heard footsteps outside the room, she sat up and watched the door.

A tall man in a navy suit and purple paisley tie entered with a file in his hand. He wore his dark hair a little long and his eyes were mesmerizing in a fierce way. His eyes held the potential for kindness—or stern judgment.

"My name is Detective Estefan Cruz." He made no attempt to shake her hand. "You're Zoey Meager, is that right?"

"Yes. That's me."

The detective read from his file, information about her. He knew where she worked, where she lived and what she drove. As he read, she glanced toward the mirror and wondered who watched her from the other side.

Paranoid much?

Out of the blue, he pulled her attention back by asking a direct question.

"What were you doing at that warehouse?" the detective asked as he slouched back in his chair. He fixed his dark eyes on her and didn't back off. "SWAT officers found you near the loading bays, unconscious. You were suffering from smoke inhalation. That means you were inside. Why?"

The man glared at her as if she were guilty of something. She took a deep breath and ignored his attitude.

"A friend of mine is missing. Kaity Boyer." She shut her eyes tight and pictured the face of her best friend. "I filed a missing person report a week ago, but no one can tell me what's going on."

The detective flinched and a flash of something dark veiled his eyes. The accusation in his gaze had vanished.

"That doesn't answer my question. Why were you at the warehouse?"

"I've been looking for Kaity. I took all my banked vacation days at work. I just have to find her."

Zoey wrapped her arms around her chest to fend off the cold. Whenever she thought about not finding Kaity, it scared her.

"I haven't slept much since she disappeared," she said. "I drive to all the places she used to hang out and I ask around. Someone told me the Bloods were into human trafficking. It scared the hell out of me, but I went to that abandoned warehouse because I heard they used it as a safe house to keep women."

"So you thought your friend, Kaity, might've been held there? Did you hear about the hostages? Dispatch got a call, reporting a hostage situation."

"No. I didn't know anything about that until Sam Riggs told me. He's a fireman out of—"

"I know who he is. Go on."

"When I got there, the place was already torched but the fire crew couldn't put out the blaze. Cops had to make sure it was safe."

"That's standard protocol." He narrowed his eyes. "So you decided to run into a burning building to look for her. That's insane."

"It seemed like a stellar idea at the time." She bit the inside of her lip. "That fire was deliberately set. Whoever did it, they used an accelerant on the first floor, near the back. I smelled it. I think I saw the guy who did it, too."

The cynical expression on the detective's face vanished. She'd poked his interest.

"What? You saw someone inside?"

Zoey told him about the man in black, how he'd tried to kill her. She told him about the snake tattoo and his bloody arm. She didn't hold back.

"I don't know how I ended up outside," she said. "I thought I'd die in that warehouse."

"You didn't know the man you claimed you saw in the building?"

"What do you mean, claimed? Why would I know—?" It took her a long moment to realize he had accused her of something. "You think I set the fire?"

"You just know a lot about where the fire had started and that an accelerant was used. I'm a cop. My brain is hard-wired for suspicion."

"That's crazy."

"In my line of work, crazy isn't so crazy."

The detective stopped taking notes. His cocky belligerence faded when he had difficulty looking her in the eye.

"Look, I hate to be the one to tell you this, but after they put out the fire, we found the bodies of three dead young women."

Zoey gasped and her eyes stung with welling tears.

"Is Kaity...I mean, was she—?" She couldn't finish. Saying the words aloud would make them real.

"The coroner hasn't identified the bodies yet. Autopsies are scheduled for today and tomorrow." The detective leaned his elbows on the table and lowered his voice. "Until you know your friend is one of them, don't borrow trouble. I'll call you when we ID them, but tell me about your friend, Kaity. What happened to her?"

Zoey fought through her misery to tell him about her friend. She told him the facts of what happened the night she was abducted. Facts were easy. They didn't punch her heart like the guilt did. She let the detective ask the questions and she answered. She gave him the names of the cops she'd spoken to, the people on the street where she gathered information, and where she'd been to look for Kaity.

"Do you believe me?" Zoey asked. "I didn't set that fire. I never would've hurt those women."

The man only stared at her and refused to answer her question. She couldn't believe she had to convince him she wasn't a murderer. When her exhaustion kicked in, so did her temper.

"Unless I'm under arrest, you have no reason to hold me."

She stood and glared at him, daring Detective Cruz to challenge her. The four walls of the interrogation room closed in on her. Like a cold-blooded reptile, Detective Cruz didn't blink, but she refused to back down from the reptile king. He'd either call her bluff or let her go. At the moment, Zoey didn't feel lucky, but she doubled down and pushed her questionable fortune.

"I'll need someone to drive me back to my car." She crossed her arms and lifted her chin.

Dead silence, but Cruz finally blinked.

"Don't leave town," he said, as he handed her one of his business cards. "Call me if you think of anything I should know."

She let out the breath she'd been holding.

Leave town? Not on your life, Detective.

Zoey had no intention of leaving Denver, not while Kaity was still missing. Cruz was only the latest detective, in a long line of law enforcement skeptics, who'd refused to help her. She wouldn't give up on a friend who was closer than a sister.

Kaity would've done the same for her. Fact.

***

Denver Police Department
Central Station
Noon

Detective Cruz took his time letting her go. By the time he wrangled a cop to drive Zoey back to her vehicle, she was starving, worn out, and mad as hell. She had parked down the street from the destroyed warehouse. After she pulled into the street, she slowed down when she drove by the building, to take it all in.

I almost died last night.

The tears on her cheeks weren't because of what could've happened to her. She cried when she thought of Kaity. One of the bodies the coroner would identify might be her best friend. She felt gut

31

punched and had nowhere else to look for Kaity if she were dead and at the morgue. Zoey had run out of bread crumbs. Now she'd have to wait for a call from Detective Cruz to let her know if her search had come to a very bad end.

"Oh, Kaity. I'd know if you were dead, wouldn't I?" she whispered.

She glanced into the rearview mirror and caught a glimpse of black raccoon eyes. Her mascara had made a mess of her face.

"Oh, great. I look like the Walking Dead."

She reached into the glove compartment of her Subaru and grabbed a packet of tissues to wipe her face, but when she looked in the mirror, she caught the glint of sunlight off glass. A man was parked a block down—sitting in a white windowless panel van—taking photos of her. His lens wasn't aimed at the burned down warehouse.

The camera had targeted her. *What the hell?*

She didn't turn around or let on she'd seen him. She tossed the tissues onto her passenger seat and started her Subaru. If he didn't follow her, the whole thing could be her imagination. After she pulled into traffic and made her first two turns, she thought she'd lost him—until the white van made the last turn and headed straight at her.

"This can't be happening."

Why would he follow *her* and take photos? Goose bumps rippled over her skin and she gripped the steering wheel tighter. Her heart raced, the beats pounding through her chest. But when she thought of the only thing that had changed—her meeting with Detective Estefan Cruz—the fear that gripped her had vanished and had turned into indignant anger.

"Not cool, Detective. If this is how you wanna play it, then game on."

She had nothing to fear from a plain clothes cop assigned to tail her. That was the only explanation. No one had known where she'd be, especially after she got picked up by the police. Detective Cruz didn't trust her.

Well, two can play that game.

Zoey hit the gas and sped around the corner. All she had to do was out-maneuver a van and lose a cop.

Chapter 4

Downtown Denver

Evening

Zoey kept her eyes on the rearview mirror and kept driving. It had been a very long day, but she hadn't given up on Kaity. Detective Cruz had been right about not borrowing trouble. Unless she knew for sure that Kaity was dead, she had to keep the faith that her best friend was still alive.

When Zoey had needed gas for her Subaru, or something to eat or drink, she'd paid in cash. Since she knew cops tracked credit card transactions, she let her paranoid flag fly high and she'd kept alert and on the move. She had retraced her steps. It's all she knew how to do.

As dusk faded into nightfall, the lights of the city turned neon. People morphed into black silhouettes without faces. If she couldn't go home—because home would make her an easy target for the cops to track her—she would have to find a place to sleep and buy a change in clothes. Whenever her cash ran out, she'd hit an ATM, but she'd deal with that when everything else played out.

With Ariana Grande's 'Dangerous Woman' playing softly on her sound system—a favorite of Kaity's—she drove through the downtown streets searching for her friend, acting as if she had eyes in the back of her head. The urban landscape of Denver metro changed to seedier streets, vacant warehouses, tattoo parlors and palm readers.

The hair on the back of her neck stood on end until something from the corner of her eye caught her full attention.

"No, it can't be."

She pulled her Subaru to the curb and parked in the closest spot, without losing sight of the diner at the corner behind her. Her heart thrashed in her chest as she leaped from her vehicle, slammed the door shut and locked it. Zoey licked her lips and slowed her pace as she came close to the entrance.

The huge black dog she'd seen at the burning warehouse. It sat on its haunches, still as stone, staring into the diner. She took in every detail. It *had* to be the same dog. She was sure of it. When she drew closer, she whispered.

"Remember me, big guy?"

People on the street stared at her as if she'd lost her mind. She knew the look and she didn't care. Seeing the dog had been too much coincidence for her to ignore.

"Why are you here?" She extended the back of her hand to let the dog have a sniff. "Are you with somebody?"

The dog barely glanced at her. He kept his massive head trained on the diner. Zoey turned to see what had the dog spellbound.

One man stood at the cash register. He had his back to her. She couldn't see his face. He filled out his jeans and had a worn jean jacket on with a hoodie underneath. The hood covered his head and made it hard to see his face from where she stood. The waitress handed him a takeout bag and he paid in cash. When he moved to pay, she saw the snake tattoo on his hand and wrist and it jolted her. The fear from last night came back in a rush.

It's him.

"Damn."

She reacted on instinct and ducked into the

shadows, keeping her eyes on the dog. There'd been a reason the animal had been at the warehouse last night. His master had tried to kill her—and maybe had started the fire that killed those women. Her throat wedged tight and she felt the burn of tears.

Maybe he had killed Kaity. *Oh, God. This can't be happening.*

Her mind raced with what to do. Her throat went dry and she wrung her hands as she stared at the dog that had no interest in her. Should she call Detective Cruz? What would she tell him? If the cops didn't get to the diner fast, the man would walk and she'd lose him. She would have nothing to tell the police, except that her mystery man—the guy Detective Cruz thought she'd invented—had a taste for 'cholesterol to go.'

She felt utterly useless, but she had to do something.

Zoey steeled her spine for what would come next, but before a plan formed in her head, the diner door swung open and the dog followed his faceless master into the shadows. Zoey peered around the corner, holding her breath, unsure what to do. She watched him until darkness swallowed him, until every ounce of love she had for Kaity welled in her throat and threatened to strangle her.

She couldn't do it. Zoey wouldn't let him get away. For Kaity's sake, she ignored the warning siren blaring in her head. She took off on foot to hunt a dangerous man, mumbling justifications under her breath.

"Just find out where he's staying and call 9-1-1. That's it." She quickened her steps to catch up to him. "Give Cruz a heads up. That's all I have to do."

Simple, right?

Yeah, real simple.

***

Five Points Historic District
Downtown Denver

The guy moved like a predator. He kept his head down, but that was only a ruse. Zoey noticed he glanced into every glass reflection, giving him eyes behind his head. He would stop unexpectedly, duck into a doorway and come out another way. No casual observer would've noticed, but she did. He kept her on her toes, forcing her to fall back and play it smarter.

Zoey watched street signs to keep track of where

he took her. When she saw landmarks for the historic Five Points area of Denver, she racked her brain remembering what she'd read about the high crime area. Local news reported a renewed rivalry between the Bloods, who'd taken over Park Hill and Five Points, and the Crips, who dominated Montbello. Gang violence was at an all-time high and she worried that Kaity had crossed paths with someone connected.

She ducked into storefronts and lingered in the shadows. She'd nearly lost him twice, which threw her into a panic until she found him again. Stalking him had been exhausting. Every second felt like an eternity, especially because of where he'd led her—into blocks of deserted buildings and ramshackle houses. She didn't make eye contact with anyone on the street. Men ogled her and she kept moving, praying.

His dog kept pace with him, sticking tight to his side. If the guy turned, the animal hit his mark and never strayed. The way the dog moved with his master reminded her of a tightly choreographed dance number or the mirror-imaging of synchronized diving. *Remarkable.*

In her exhaustion, she let her mind wander and

in that split second, she lost him again. This time she tried to stay calm, but when the treacherous neighborhood overwhelmed her, Zoey panicked.

"Oh, no." She gasped. "No, no, no. Where the hell did you go?"

She quickened her steps and raced to a corner, easing up to it with her back to the wall, and peered down the street.

He'd vanished, dog and all.

"No!" She stomped her foot and clenched her teeth. Zoey spun on her heels and looked up and down the road, into the windows overhead, and ran down the block—nothing.

"Damn it."

Her predicament sent chills racing across her skin. She stood in the middle of a horror show. The alley he'd led her through was long and narrow, lined with trash and broken glass. A Dumpster reeked of rotting food and puke, and something dead.

She hadn't given her safety a second thought. After she'd lost him, every shadow played tricks on her eyes and moved in the dark. She took shelter near a trash bin and listened for footsteps, or any noise that warned her she wasn't alone.

"Who are you?" A low gravelly voice came from

behind her.

Zoey jumped and screamed. With her heart hammering, she spun with her fists tight, ready to punch him.

"Stay back. Don't come any closer," she threatened. When her voice cracked, she winced. "I saw you at the warehouse. You tried to kill me."

"I don't know what you're talking about." He stepped out of the shadows. Zoey couldn't see his eyes or most of his face. "You don't belong here. It's dangerous for someone like you."

"I can handle myself."

His lip curled into a dismissive smile. If she had blinked, she would've missed it.

"If you say so."

For a split second, she noticed the glint of sweat across his upper lip. Something in his body language or the pallor of his skin sent her a message. As a nurse, she knew how to read sick people. She inched closer to him to play a hunch, with every fiber of her body shivering inside.

"Are you saying you weren't at the warehouse that burned down?" She didn't wait for him to answer. "Then how would I know you have a snake tattoo on your wrist?"

"I don't have to confirm or deny." He sighed. "Go home, whoever you are."

When he turned to go, she grabbed for his arm. He cried out in pain and pulled from her grasp. She'd been right. He *had* been shot or stabbed.

"Your wound could be infected. You have a fever, don't you?" She didn't back down. "I'm a nurse. I can help you."

"I don't need your help. Leave me alone."

He turned his back on her and walked down the alley into the shadows. His dog sprang from the dark and raced to his side, as if they had one mind.

"You have no idea how stubborn I am," Zoey yelled after him. "I'm coming back here tomorrow. I'll have meds and gauze and sterile dressing."

He didn't say another word and disappeared like mist into the dark.

Zoey didn't know why she'd offered to help him, until she realized that if she got close enough—if he let his guard down—she could take something from him with his fingerprints on it. Detective Cruz would have to believe her.

Once and for all she'd find out why he had been at the warehouse. He could be her only lifeline to Kaity.

***

Hours later

Zoey's feet ached from all the walking. She wanted to make a beeline back to her car, but she'd gotten lost twice. The dog whisperer had led her through a maze he knew well, but she didn't. She roamed the streets until landmarks looked familiar and she stuck to the shadows, avoiding anyone on two legs.

Zoey trudged up the last street, Broadway, dragging her bacon. When she saw the diner sign still lit—On the Corner—she picked up her pace. Her only thought was to get in her car, find a reasonable motel, and take a long hot shower.

But when she walked past the diner, she saw the same waitress who had cashed out her mystery man. Without a second of hesitation, she yanked open the door and stepped into the place as if she'd been there many times.

"Be with you in a minute, honey. Sit anywhere you like." The waitress smiled and the etched lines on her face folded like an accordion playing a polka. She looked like someone Zoey would like to call friend.

The diner was a throwback to the fifties with its red vinyl booths, black and white tiled floor, and chrome finishes. A counter stretched the length of the diner, along the kitchen serving window, with spinning stools for people who dined alone or wanted to read the paper without interruption. It smelled of pies, burgers, fresh coffee, and a Bruce Springsteen classic played on a vintage jukebox. The patrons were an odd mix of the elderly, body builders, and hookers. *Real homey.*

Zoey slid into the closest booth, away from the nearest ears, and waited for the woman she'd come to see.

"We're out of the special, but there are plenty more good things on the menu. Take a look." The waitress handed her a plastic covered list of offerings. She wore a black T-shirt with the diner's name across the front—On the Corner—with jeans, sneakers, and an apron with pockets. A badge bore her name, Charlotte.

Zoey leaned into the table and lowered her voice.

"You know anything about the guy with the black dog? He was in here earlier."

It took Charlotte only a moment to recall.

"Oh, you mean Mr. January?" She shrugged.

"Not a thing, except for what's important."

"What does *that* mean?"

"It means his dog eats better than he does, honey. He buys a burger, but his dog gets steak." She grinned and winked. "You can tell a lot about a man who knows how to take care of his dog."

Low and gravelly, Charlotte's voice made her sound gruff, but the twinkle and mischief in her eyes made Zoey smile.

"Why do you call him, Mr. January? Is that his real name?"

The waitress blushed and grabbed a damp rag off a nearby workstation. She wiped down Zoey's table as a distraction. Blotches of red colored the pale skin on Charlotte's cheeks and down her neck. A shy smile transformed her face and made her look years younger.

"If I were doing a calendar of gorgeous men, he would be my January man," she whispered.

Charlotte heaved a sigh and stared out the darkened windows of the diner.

"A woman needs someone to melt the chill in the dead of winter," she said. "He's cool on the outside, but smoking hot where it counts. He would be my Mr. January. Now what can I get you?"

She ignored the woman's question.

"Do you have any idea where he lives?"

"Not a clue. Why?" She narrowed her eyes.

"No reason." Zoey had never been a very good liar. The woman smirked and gave her a motherly look.

"Sometimes wild things need to stay untamed, honey. He doesn't strike me as someone who should be or wants to be domesticated. That one's a loner, certified." Her face softened in sympathy. "He could be dangerous. Just because I have fantasies about him being calendar worthy, doesn't mean he's okay for someone like you. You look like a sweet girl, but Mr. January has a razor sharp edge to him. My two cents, for whatever it's worth."

Zoey didn't know what to make of Mr. January. He scared the hell out of her, lived like a homeless man, and had tried to kill her. He'd been hurt and didn't go to a doctor. Only criminals did that. Gunshots or stabbings would get reported to police. If Charlotte thought he was dangerous, taking care of a dog didn't put him in the zip code of normal.

She handed back her menu and grinned.

"I'll have breakfast. The works...and coffee. I'm suddenly hungry."

After Charlotte took her order and left, Zoey stared at her reflection in the window. She looked exhausted with a pinch of maniacal. She ran a hand through her straight dark hair, but nothing helped. She needed sleep and a good soak, but one thought lingered and carried weight.

She believed in fate.

Zoey had driven by this diner at the exact right time for a reason. She saw the dog. *His* dog. The guy ate at the On the Corner diner on Broadway. Zoey would find a motel nearby and tomorrow she would do as she promised and bring medical supplies.

She'd trust her gut and she would hunt for Mr. January. He's all she had.

Chapter 5

Department of Environmental Health
Office of the Medical Examiner
Next afternoon

Detective Estefan Cruz walked through the sliding glass doors at the entrance to the governmental offices off Bannock Road, with its sleek blue glass and stone exterior. He knew his way through the maze of the impressive 100,000 square-foot crime investigation and forensics labs and headed for the third floor with his hands full of Starbucks goodies.

Cruz remembered when the coroner's office had been located next to St. Joseph's Hospital, but when the accommodations became cramped, the city built the new premiere institute off Bannock. At the old location, a banner day might be six autopsies. With the new state-of-the-art facility, they could do up to sixteen, which made a difference with mass casualties.

"I got you a double shot espresso and a blueberry scone," Cruz said to the man he'd come to see. "I know how you need a late afternoon pick-me-up."

Coroner, Dr. Jeffrey Baxter, wore his full white spatter gear with blue latex gloves. The man's eyes lit up as he smiled under his mask.

"Aw. You're a good man, Detective. Thank you."

Cruz placed the coffee and the pastry bag on a counter near the sliding glass doors. The autopsy bay glistened in stainless. A bank of refrigeration units, used for body storage, ran along the perimeter of the room. The coroner had one body in front of him covered in a white sheet. Tools of his trade were gleaming on a cart with wheels next to the autopsy table—a bone saw, rib cutters, skull chisel, and a Stryker saw that would be used to remove the brain.

The doctor pulled back the sheet and exposed the face of one of the young women who died in the warehouse fire. She had soot caked inside her nostrils and her lips were tinged in black. Her face and eyes were swollen.

"Will you be staying?" Dr. Baxter asked.

"I can't think of a better way to spend my day than observing three 'Y' incisions by you, Doc, but no. Not today. Just give me the Cliff Notes."

The coroner gave his preliminary findings based on his initial observations. Cruz made notes of key elements. Cause of death appeared to be smoke inhalation. Ligature marks on the wrists and ankles were made by barbed wire. The women had been locked in a storage unit and the arson investigator had found evidence of arson with an accelerant used. The coroner expected to find tissue hypoxia from the absorption of poisonous toxins like carbon monoxide and cyanide.

"Any ID?" the detective asked.

"We ran fingerprints on all three victims and got hits. I printed their records for you."

"Thanks, doc." He flipped through the file the coroner had made for him. "Kaity Boyer wasn't one of them?"

"Did you expect her to be?"

"No, but someone did." Cruz raised the file and said, "Thanks, Doc. Shoot me finals when you have them."

"After the lab work is back, I'll do that." The coroner smiled. "Say hello to that lovely wife of yours."

"I don't have a wife, doc."

"Well, you better get on that." He grinned.

Cruz only shook his head, but as he headed out of autopsy, he thought of Zoey Meager. She would be happy to hear her friend wasn't part of the collateral damage, but the Boyer girl was still missing and the case had grown ice cold. He hadn't bought Zoey's mystery guy story. It sounded like a distraction from the real question of why she'd been found on the premises of an arson fire.

On a hunch, he grabbed his cell and called Detective Dravin.

"Hey, Dravin. You get any hits on the barbed wire ligatures?"

"Yeah, just now. Looks like we have a network of human traffickers with a conduit through Colorado and Wyoming, but here's the clincher," Dravin said. Cruz heard paper rustling in the background. "ViCAP had two vics in Denver and three in Pueblo, all of them killed in arson fires. Sounds like our traffickers have a pipeline along I-25 and a thing for arson. It destroys witnesses and evidence."

"Yeah, thanks. Good work." He ended the call with his mind reeling with questions as he punched a button on the elevator, heading for the ground floor.

With other linked cases having barbed wire ligatures and the signature MO of killing women by arson fire, Cruz knew it would be less likely that Zoey Meager had anything to do with the warehouse fire, but he didn't like the way she held back from him. He understood that she didn't trust cops when it came to her best friend, but her dangerous slant toward becoming a vigilante made him wonder what she was hiding.

The cop who took her missing person report thought she'd hidden something, too. He'd written at the bottom of the paperwork, the letters JDLR and circled them for the next cop to see. That was cop speak for 'just doesn't look right.' Yeah, that was a thing cops did. They made up code that became universal, passed from cop to cop. Cruz had spoken to the cop who'd written the initials to ask why he'd made the note. The officer shared his thoughts.

'She was sketchy on how she knew her girlfriend was in trouble when I found out later that she wasn't even at the bar where the girl was last seen. It's like she was making stuff up to sound worse than what it was, to get us to make her friend's case a top priority.'

Cruz had the gut feeling she held something back, too. Zoey had told him she'd heard rumors of a gang that was into trafficking girls. Had she made that up? When he hadn't found a gang connection, he had the suspicion she might have embellished her story to move it up their caseload. But if what she'd said about her mystery man in the warehouse had been the truth, he had a person of interest to question. Maybe *he* could connect the dots.

Cruz had to find Zoey.

***

Downtown Denver

Hanging out all day at a Dumpster turned out *not* to be a stellar plan.

Come on. You need me. I know you do.

Zoey pleaded in her head with the faceless man, the one with the chilling deep voice. Her mental ramblings had become her mantra and as the hours wore on, she spoke to him as if he were with her.

Infections are serious. You can't ignore them. You have to trust me. I know stuff.

Stashed in a backpack, she'd brought medical supplies to treat his wound and a few other store-bought things, but what guy turned down medical help when he needed it? A criminal, a guy with secrets, that's who. Her better judgment played devil's advocate without relenting. She knew her impulsive actions might get her neck deep in trouble, but she had to try.

I have to do this for Kaity.

In daylight she had retraced the steps she'd taken while trailing Mr. January last night. She'd used her senses to confirm which Dumpster. As a nurse, she'd seen her share of puke and could target it at fifty paces. From the garbage bin she took off on foot and followed where he might've gone from there.

Epic fail.

After she returned to her car, she powered up her phone and checked her cell for messages. She'd had her cell off because she didn't want the police to use her GPS to find her. Detective Cruz had called five times, but left only one voice mail. Her fingers raced across the keys to listen to his message. She didn't know what he would say, but if he had any word on Kaity, she had to know. Zoey listened to Cruz's gruff, no nonsense voice on the recording.

'The bodies we found at the warehouse fire, none of them were your friend, Kaity Boyer. She's

still in the wind, but I have questions on the guy you claimed was inside the warehouse, the one you think you saw. Can you come to Central Station to work with a sketch artist?'

The man's words dripped with condescension. He didn't believe her the other day and time hadn't improved his attitude.

"You're only dangling a carrot because I ditched the cop you sent to tail me. You want a second shot at me."

If the detective decided to hold her for questioning, or on suspicion of being involved in the arson, she could be held for three days—or worse.

No way. Not gonna happen.

Zoey had to rely on her instincts now. Cops could stop her from searching for Kaity. She couldn't let that happen.

Before she turned off her phone, she listened to Kaity's recorded message one more time, the last time she heard her friend's voice. It ravaged her heart and punished her, abuse she deserved. Guilt drove her, but love—and her desperate need to have a second chance with a friend she thought of as a sister—had consumed her life.

Zoey wiped tears from her face and turned off

her phone before she started her Subaru. She drove back to the area where she'd found the trash Dumpster. She dared to drive through the labyrinths of dilapidated warehouses in a part of Denver she'd never been, before last night. Zoey had her doors locked and eyes alert as she searched for Mr. January and his dog, but it was getting dark. After the sun went down, everything would get complicated and more dangerous.

***

Downtown Denver

After 7:00 pm

The sun abandoned the day and sank in defeat beneath the skyline. Its retreat made dark ominous silhouettes of the towering warehouses she drove through and a chill closed in. Zoey felt trounced and exhausted. Her stomach grumbled in protest. When she found herself near the garbage bin where she'd started her day, she indulged her gut instinct and turned into the alley and parked.

Something moved in the shadows.

Zoey tightened her grip on the steering wheel as she peered through the windshield into the beam of her headlights. With a hand on the gear shift, she nearly put her Subaru in Reverse and hit the gas, until something made her stay.

When her headlights reflected off a pair of familiar dark eyes, her heart pounded faster. *His dog.* The big black animal crept toward her with head low and staring. She eased the vehicle door open and stood behind it, unsure if she should step out.

"Good boy. Where's your master?" She reached into the car, not taking her eyes off the dog, and retrieved her rucksack. "Show me where he is? Is he sick, boy?"

The words were out of her mouth before she realized they rang with truth. Somehow she knew she'd guessed right. His dog had waited for her to return because his master was in trouble. She threw the backpack over her shoulder, locked her car, and focused on the dog.

"Take me to him," she whispered. "Show me where he is, boy."

The dog circled where it stood and whined. When she drew closer, the animal took off down the alley, only stopping and circling again if she didn't keep up.

"I'm coming. I'm coming." She hoisted the

shoulder straps of the heavy pack and picked up her pace.

She followed the clicks of the dog's nails on asphalt in the dark, wishing she'd thought to bring a flashlight. The animal made three turns, never faltering, and stopped at a fire escape. He looked back once and yelped before he climbed the stairs and sat on his haunches at the top landing.

"What's it gonna be, Zoey?" she asked under her breath. "A genius move or the dumbest thing you've ever done?"

She didn't feel lucky. Zoey took a deep breath, gripped the metal rail and climbed. Whatever the answer would be, she'd have to crawl through the window of a place suitable for the Unabomber and find out.

After she got to the top landing, the dog didn't budge. He sat and wagged his tail, but never tried to crawl through the window before her.

Zoey straddled the sill and tossed her bag to the floor. It took too many precious seconds to see anything in the dark cavernous space. In a far corner, she saw a flickering candle. It cast eerie shadows across the brick walls as she eased through the window.

She sensed something in the room—*someone.*

Zoey held her breath and inched toward the sputtering candle and a mattress on the floor. Someone moved under a sheet and groaned. She gripped the straps of the rucksack, ready to swing it as a weapon, as she stepped closer.

A man thrashed under dank bed sheets. His bare muscled chest glistened with sweat. He looked delirious and mumbled in his fevered sleep. His thick dark hair looked drenched and he had a day's growth of stubble. The wound on his arm looked swollen and had turned an angry red with infection. The bullet hole had started bleeding again.

Her throat went bone dry and her heart punished her ribcage as she knelt by him. She reached out her trembling fingers and touched his face. He was burning up.

"Are you...okay?" She didn't know if she said the words aloud and tried again, a little louder. "Remember me? I came back. Are you—?"

The man moved with lightning speed and reached under his pillow. Zoey came face-to-face with a gun pointed between her eyes and she gasped. His fierce dark eyes stared at her and his hand shook with the fever under his skin.

Zoey didn't move.

She didn't breathe.

Chapter 6

Downtown Denver

7:40 pm

A tear ran down Zoey's cheek as she stared into the barrel of his gun. She didn't want to die.

Please don't do this.

Anger flashed over his face and he mumbled something in Spanish. Wherever he was, he wasn't with her or at the warehouse. The infection had him a world away and Zoey had no idea how to get him to see her.

"I'm not who you think I am," she begged with her hands raised. "You're sick. You have a fever."

"Cállate!" he shouted, panting with the exertion.

His eyes drooped and the gun trembled in his big hand.

"I'm a nurse. I'm here to help you."

His eyes softened and his face went slack. When his chin dropped to his chest, he slumped back onto the mattress and passed out with the gun still in his hand. Zoey reached for the weapon with shaky fingers and slid it from his grasp. Her whole body shook when the worst was over.

After she found a safe place to hide his gun, she got to work and unzipped her backpack.

She would stop the bleeding, clean and dress the wound, give him meds for the infection, then do her best to bathe him, but nothing would be easy. The fever had a hold on him. He thrashed under her care. Zoey had to press her weight against him, to hold him down while she tended to his injured arm. She didn't know if he was naked under the sheet and tried not to dwell on his impressive body.

But he fought every touch she made.

Worn out from the struggle, Zoey finally pulled away from him to search the room for other things she'd need. She found his stash of clothes and used a T-shirt to soak in water at a utility sink. She ran the wet cloth down his muscular chest and taut stomach to cool him off. When he quit fighting her, he fell into a deep sleep. For the first time, Zoey allowed herself to hope that she'd gotten to him in time and he'd be okay.

The black dog crawled onto the foot of the mattress and nestled his chin on the leg of his sleeping master. A low rumbling whine broke the silence in the room and with big watery eyes, the dog stared at her.

"You did the right thing, boy." She reached out a hand and stroked the dog's head, running her fingers through his soft fur. "I'm here now. Everything's gonna be okay."

Zoey watched Mr. January sleep. Everything would be okay—until he woke up.

He'll wake up...eventually. Then what?

Her eyes grew wide when she thought of what he might do. She had his gun, but a big man like Mr. January could hurt her or kill her with his bare hands. He didn't need a weapon. Zoey would have him docile for only a short time. She had to act fast if she wanted answers for Kaity.

By candlelight, she reached for her phone and looked up the number she had programmed into her cell for Detective Estefan Cruz. She'd added his name to her directory, along with all the other Denver police officers who'd given her empty promises on Kaity.

Zoey made up her mind on what had to be done. She grabbed what she needed and headed for the fire escape, but before she left, she looked over her shoulder to the sick man on the bed.

"Sorry. I have to do this," she whispered, and crawled through the window.

***

Denver County Fair Grounds
8:30 pm

The cryptic text message Detective Cruz received from Zoey Meager twenty minutes ago had intrigued him, but when he tried to call her, the infuriating woman had turned off her phone. He had only one chance to get this right and she didn't leave him any time.

The place would close at 9:00 pm.

He hit the gas pedal, speeding down I-70 as he headed for the Denver County Fair Grounds. Up ahead he saw the colorful lights of the lit Ferris wheels and the rainbow neon of the Midway. He turned onto a side street that led to the livestock exhibits. When he saw the sign for 'Bulls,' he parked near the loading bay entrance and grabbed his cell phone to read her instructions once more.

Livestock Exhibit - Bulls
Go to stall 32 – Charolais "Joe Cocker"

Under the SPERM FOR SALE sign, I've left you something you want. Run the fingerprints and I'll contact you tomorrow for everything you have on him. If you want him, you'll do as I ask.

When he walked into the exhibit hall for bulls, he winced at the smell. The stench of bull shit had him cursing Zoey Meager under his shallow breaths. He followed the numbered stalls and found 'Joe Cocker.' The enormous white Charolais bull with its wet, slimy snout huffed in its pen. The animal's owners were selling his sperm and had a poster advertising it.

The detective found a plastic bag tucked behind the sign. In the bag was a flattened, discarded water bottle. He looked at it in the light and noticed the smudges of fingerprints.

"Did it have to be a 'sperm for sale' sign, Zoey?"

Cruz gave a thought to ask what the sperm sold for, but decided against the humiliation of knowing a bull named Joe Cocker made serious coin off his calf batter.

The detective headed back to his car. By tomorrow, with any luck, he would have the identity of the man Zoey had taken the fingerprints from. Had she found the guy in the warehouse on her own? If she had gone vigilante on him, Cruz didn't want to think of the danger she could be in. Or maybe she wanted to throw suspicion on someone else.

Either way, Zoey Meager hadn't given him any more reason to trust her. Tomorrow he would issue a BOLO alert. The entire Denver police force would 'be on lookout' for her and her vehicle. He'd track her credit card and ATM use, too. Cruz had to tighten the noose and bring her back in for questioning. He couldn't allow her to use him and the resources of the DPD—not on his watch.

***

Hours later

Zoey paced the warehouse floor, watching Mr. January sleep. Whenever he tossed and turned from the fever, she cooled his body down with a wet rag. She touched his hot brow and prayed his fever would break soon. When he needed more medicine, she woke him enough to lift his head, give him pills, and make sure he drank water.

In the flickering candlelight, he stared up at her, but he didn't question why she'd come. Zoey wasn't sure he remembered her, but the intimacy of taking care of him had satisfied them both. If Kaity hadn't been in trouble and Zoey had met him under different circumstances, she might be looking at her next mistake. She zeroed in on guys who needed fixing or they found her. She'd always been a sucker for dark, brooding men, but add a hard body and fierce eyes that brimmed with mystery, and she was a goner. His full lips were a bonus.

What are you doing, Zoey? The man is unconscious and most likely a criminal.

Zoey sighed. The guy definitely had it all. The way his hair curled at the nape of his neck turned her on, utterly finger-worthy. After what she'd seen of his narrow waist and hips, she pictured her favorite part of the male anatomy—the small of his back and the gentle curve of his butt. Fantasizing helped her pass the time, but her physical attraction to him had to be shoved aside.

She knelt by him and ran her fingers through his hair, taking in the handsome face of a stranger—a man who might know something about her friend. She pictured Kaity scared, alone and in danger and she fought the burn of tears.

You have to help me. Please.

Time stopped while she cared for him and she felt too wired to close her eyes and rest. After his fever had gone down and he slept, she wandered to the window and sat on the sill. She stared into the night sky and her thoughts turned to her friend. Cruz had said Kaity wasn't one of the bodies in the morgue, but that didn't mean she was safe. Zoey's belly tightened whenever she thought of the horrors happening to Kaity.

In the quiet of the cold warehouse, taking care of a dangerous stranger, she never felt so alone. *I'll find you, Kates. I will. I have to.*

When a car alarm sounded in the night, it jolted her back to her senses. The jarring noise echoed off the brick walls in the canyon of warehouses below. When she realized the alarm had to be her Subaru, she rushed to her feet, grabbed her car keys, and her cell phone.

No. You can't call 9-1-1. No GPS, remember?

She stuffed her phone back into her jeans and after she checked on Mr. January one last time, she

68

slipped out of the window and headed down the fire escape.

What are you gonna do when you get there, big shot?

She thought she was alone until she heard the familiar clicking of her big black shadow. Mr. January's dog had come with her.

"Good boy. Thank you."

She ran through the alley, remembering the turns she had made earlier. When she got to her Subaru, two men had jimmied the locks and were sitting in her car. Improvising, she grabbed her phone and put it to her ear.

"Yes, two men are breaking into my car. You want their descriptions?" She held her phone toward the man in her car. "I can take a picture. Smile guys. Ever hear of facial recognition?"

When the black dog growled and crept toward the men with his head hanging low and threatening, the two thieves yelled something in Spanish and ran. They never looked back.

"They must be photo shy." Zoey knelt down and ruffled the fur on the dog's neck. "Thank you, big guy. You saved my bacon. You feel like taking a ride?"

She couldn't leave her car where it was. With her

companion in the passenger seat, she drove to On the Corner on Broadway, the diner where she'd first seen Mr. January the other night. The restaurant was opening for its early breakfast patrons. Another waitress helped her find a secure spot to park her vehicle and took her order-to-go for breakfast.

As she walked back to the warehouse, with Mr. January's dog, she turned on her phone and called Detective Cruz.

"Cruz." His stern voice made her cringe.

"It's Zoey. Did you get an ID on those prints I left for you?"

"Where did you get them, Ms. Meager?"

"Answer me first, or I hang up."

Silence. Zoey smiled at him calling her Ms. Meager. She had him over a barrel, whether he wanted to admit it or not.

"However you acquired these prints, you're dealing with a dangerous man, Ms. Meager. I can't even give you his name. He's a ghost. His file is blocked, but it has a warning on it. The Feds are on their way here to give me a pee pee sanding. They'll want to know where he is. For the hassle factor alone, you owe me."

"I don't know you well enough to do guilt,

Detective. I only do that with people I love. Nice try."

"Wait. Don't hang up. There's something else you should know. You're not going to like it."

"What's that?"

"The dead women in the warehouse, they were bound with a distinctive ligature, barbed wire. And as you guessed, the fire had been deliberately set. It was arson. That's the MO of the killers behind a human trafficking ring in Colorado. Whenever they are done with their victims, they get rid of the evidence with a fire. Mr. No Name could be connected to these traffickers."

He softened his voice and said her first name.

"Zoey. I'm not saying this to scare you, but you need to appreciate the risky situation you're in. If your friend Kaity has been taken by these men, she could already be dead. You could be putting yourself in danger for no reason."

"I've got a *good* reason, Detective. I do."

She ended the call and turned off her phone. If the police didn't know more than she did about where Kaity was, she couldn't leave her friend in their hands. She had to believe that the sick man, with an infection from a bullet wound, had been in the burning warehouse for a purpose.

She *had* to get him to let down his guard.

***

10:40 am

When she stroked his forehead, Mr. January was cool to the touch. His fever had broken while she'd been gone. She smiled and let out the breath she held whenever she laid a hand on his body.

Before she ate, Zoey dampened a cloth and ran the rag over his bare chest and down his stomach and arms. She dabbed his face as she watched him sleep. He had a healthier color and he didn't strain to breathe. She would change his dressing after he woke up. Zoey wanted a reason to stay, an argument she could use if he tried to kick her out.

He has to help me. I won't give him a choice.

Zoey fed his dog and made sure the animal had fresh water. After she ate her takeout from the diner—two egg and bacon breakfast tacos with salsa—she set aside the broth soup she had bought for Mr. January. She hoped he'd be hungry when he opened his eyes.

"What the hell?" His deep voice raised the hair on her neck when he broke the silence in the old warehouse.

Zoey turned to see him reach under his pillow, looking for his weapon.

"I put your gun somewhere safe."

"In case you missed it, I never invited you here."

"Are you always this grumpy with people who save your life?" She crossed her arms.

Mr. January looked at the clean bandage on his arm and saw the meds and a damp cloth next to his mattress.

"My name's Zoey Meager. And you are?"

"I'm..." When the man raised his bed sheet and looked underneath, he glared at her with fierce skepticism. "I'm naked."

"I had nothing to do..." She waggled a finger at him. "...with that."

"And yet you are fully aware."

Zoey's cheeks burned. *Busted.*

"Okay. Yeah, I may have..." She shrugged. "...been aware. But I'm a nurse. I've seen plenty of—"

Zoey scrunched her face.

"That didn't come out right."

When Mr. January tried to get out of bed, he didn't make it very far. He looked queasy and pale. She jumped at the chance to change the subject.

"Are you hungry? I brought you soup. Nothing fancy, just chicken and noodle from On the Corner on Broadway."

When she deliberately mentioned the diner, he scowled at her, but he didn't confirm or deny he knew the restaurant.

"I appreciate your help, but I didn't ask for it," he said.

"I'm not helping you without getting something in return."

"Oh? You don't exactly have the high ground in this negotiation."

"Just hear me out," she said. "You owe me *that* much."

He glared at her, but he didn't argue.

"My friend Kaity Boyer is missing. I think she's been abducted by traffickers. People I trust have told me so." She stepped closer to his bed and knelt on a corner of his mattress. From the annoyed look on his face, he didn't appreciate her invasion of his space.

"I must've passed out, the night of the fire," she said. "But I thought you were going to kill me."

He shook his head in disbelief.

"Well, apparently you were wrong. You're still breathing."

His gall at her accusation made her think twice about what she would say next. Zoey played a hunch and took a risk. She didn't remember everything from the fire. Her memory had gaps where she'd lost consciousness, but if he'd been there, he would know what happened.

"You were the one who dragged me out of the warehouse when I passed out. You saved my life. You could've let me die in the fire, like the three women they found."

"There were others?" He shut his eyes and heaved a deep sigh. Mr. January looked sick. "I didn't know."

"Who shot you? I didn't see anyone else." She regretted asking that question the minute the words left her lips.

Silence.

"You said you want something from me in return. What is it?" he asked. "I don't exactly feel long on conversation."

"I need your help to find Kaity. If you helped me get out of the warehouse alive, you must not be part of the traffickers who took her. Please nod if I'm right."

"What answer will get you to leave?"

"This isn't funny. Not to me."

His expression softened and his eyes warmed with sympathy.

"Tell me about Kaity," he said. "What happened to her?"

Zoey forced a smile when he opened a door for her to tell her friend's story. She shared everything she had told the police—even adding how she'd phoned detectives like a stalker and camped out in their waiting area until she knew they had nothing to help her—but when she was done with her story, he shrugged.

"What aren't you telling me?" he asked.

He rattled every fiber of her being. When she heard that question coming from a wary man who would know if she lied, Zoey couldn't breathe. The police didn't question anything. They took her statement, filled out a missing person report, and dropped it onto a pile of filing. What more did he want to know?

You want my darkest secret. You need me to bleed for you.

"What are you talking about? I've told you everything I said to the cops."

"You told me the facts, the easy stuff. What have

76

you left out? What didn't you tell the cops?"

He narrowed his eyes, but he didn't say another word. He stared into her soul as if he had every right to invade her heart. Zoey swallowed, hard. She tried gazing back with the same conviction, but her eyes welled with tears until gravity won and exposed her shame. The weight of her burden had become too much to bear. She pressed a hand to her lips and shut her eyes.

"I was supposed to go with her that night. She shouldn't have been alone. If we were together, maybe—" She fought the tremble in her lips whenever she thought about what she could've done to save Kaity.

The intensity of Mr. January's eyes faded, but he didn't bail her out. She'd braced for him to stop her, but he did the one thing she hadn't been prepared for—he listened.

"Kaity doesn't have family. She never knew her parents. We're kindred spirits who happened to find each other in the foster care system. She's my family, the only one who loves me, but I should've been a better person."

Zoey clutched her arms around her as a shiver of guilt tingled down her spine.

"I told her to go on, that I'd meet her at the bar. I said I had things to do." She wiped her face. "But that wasn't exactly true. I lied."

Zoey had never said the words aloud. She knew how petty she would sound to this man—how utterly shallow and childish—but if she wanted him to trust her, she had to tell him the ugly truth. Her insecurities were real. The fact that Kaity had been abducted, because of her inadequacies, made her feel worse. She hated herself for what happened.

If Kaity died, Zoey didn't deserve to be happy, ever.

"I know this will sound silly, but it's the raw, honest truth. I'm insecure about the way I look. I always have been. Before my mother drank herself to death, she took out her anger on me. She called me terrible names that a kid shouldn't have to hear. That's no excuse for how I turned out. It's just part of the baggage I live with."

"I'm sorry you had to—"

"I didn't tell you about her to get sympathy. If I could turn back the clock and wish my mother away, I'm not sure I would. I'd be a different person and I'm just getting to know who I am, but Kaity didn't deserve the trouble she's in because of my problems."

"What happened? Tell me."

"You have to understand, Kaity is prettier than I am, inside and out. Men love her. Women want to be her. Most days I can deal with her being perfect and I'm happy for her, but that night, I—"

The expression on his face changed. It had been so subtle that she might've missed it if she hadn't been watching him.

"What?" She pointed at his face. "You did an eyebrow thing and you smirked."

"I can assure you. I do *not* smirk. I'm incapable."

"Don't underestimate yourself."

"Funny. That's exactly what I was thinking...about *you*." He cocked his head. "Go on."

Her cheeks burned with embarrassment. Had he paid her a compliment?

"I didn't think she'd miss me if I didn't show to her happy hour party. I thought she'd have other friends there, but I found out she wanted to surprise me. It was meant to be only the two of us. We used to do this thing, celebrating the day we became best friends. She hadn't remembered our little ritual over the last few years, but I guess she wanted to make it up to me."

"If you didn't meet her, how do you know what

she had planned?"

He'd been listening. He figured it out.

"She left me two messages on my cell. The first one she told me about her surprise. She sounded hurt that I didn't show, but the second one is the message I can't stop listening to."

Zoey inched closer to him until she shared one of his pillows at her back and nestled against his shoulder. Her brain told her to keep her guard up, but she was about to open a vein and bleed for him. She couldn't let anything stand in the way of helping Kaity, not even her good sense. She forced her fingers to work as she replayed the voice mail from Kaity. She turned up the volume, knowing it would echo and sound worse in the deserted warehouse.

'Zoey, I'm in trouble.'

Kaity's urgent, terrified whisper gave Zoey the chills. The fear in her voice reached out to her, making her sick with a haunting agony.

'They're coming for me. If you get this message, call the police. Have them trace my phone. I'll keep it on if—'

A bone-chilling scream made Zoey jump. Tears ran down her face as she heard Kaity being terrorized. Men laughed in the background as her scared friend begged for her life. She must've dropped her phone, because someone else picked it up.

Zoey braced for the man's cruel voice that she'd heard replayed countless times.

'Don't come looking for your friend. She's mine now.'

Kaity's phone went dead and the cops had nothing to trace. When the recording ended, Zoey shook with sobs that shuddered through her body. Numb with fear, she didn't realize he had put an arm around her.

"She left messages for me and I didn't even check my phone until the next morning. By that time it was too late." She cried. "She needed me and I did *nothing.*"

She collapsed into his arms and let go. Zoey didn't hold back. If she let her mind take over, she would've pulled away from him, knowing she didn't deserve to be consoled. What happened to Kaity had been her punishment.

But nestled into the warmth of his chest, she felt safe for the first time in her life. He stroked her hair and rocked her in his arms.

"I'm sorry," she said. "I didn't mean to—"

Zoey dared to meet his gaze. She found something distant and forsaken in his somber face. Mr. January stared into the murky emptiness of his isolation. She felt a connection to him, even though he hadn't shared anything about his life—not even his name. He had an intimate way of listening. His eyes conveyed more than words ever could.

"Guilt can be gut wrenching." She sobbed. "Especially when I deserve to feel bad."

"We all have demons," he said. "There aren't enough lifetimes to escape the mistakes I made."

She sensed he drifted into a past only he held a passport to enter. He held his pain close to his heart. Whatever had happened to him, it must've been bad.

"I knew you'd understand," she said. "You want to talk about it?"

He shook his head and stared at his dog, petting the animal on the head.

"No. Some mistakes are beyond fixing."

"But not for Kaity, not if she's still alive." She touched his bare chest with her hand. "I need your help to find her. She's all I have. If you know something about her, or the people who took her, I'm begging you to help. You wouldn't have been in that warehouse if you didn't know something. We crossed paths for a reason. Even if I don't deserve it, say 'yes' to Kaity. Please."

This time it was Mr. January who couldn't look Zoey in the eye.

"How sure are you that she was trafficked? You said people you trusted told you, but—"

"What are you saying?"

He clenched his jaw.

"Look, you need to hear this. You're risking your life when she might already be dead. Her body could be in a shallow grave and you might not ever find her."

"No. That's not true. I'd know it if she were dead."

"This isn't the movies, Zoey. You don't always get a happy ending because you want one. Lousy endings are my specialty." He glared at her. "Go home. People who cross my path turn up dead."

"No. I don't believe that. You can help. I know you can."

His eyes flashed with anger.

"Get out while you're still breathing. Now!"

His dog growled, low and menacing, reminding her that the animal had only one master. She gathered her things—leaving the pills and medical supplies behind—and crawled out the window and down the fire escape. She didn't want to cry when she thought about how she'd failed Kaity again, but her tears were terrible listeners.

Zoey never felt so alone.

***

Downtown Denver

1:20 pm

Clive Barnwell sat behind the wheel of a windowless van, parked down a side street. When Zoey emerged from an alley and headed north, he pulled out his binoculars to confirm he'd found her. She'd been cagey.

"Hey, wake up. She's on the move," he said over his shoulder.

His partner groaned and farted.

"Oh, hell no, man. You're making my eyes water." He winced and rolled down the window. "Get up, Frank. It's time to work."

He'd learned his lesson not to take things for granted when it came to the girl. She was more street smart than she looked. She'd forced him to change vehicles and place a fake company name for a floral shop on the van's side panel to throw her off.

Before he started his engine, he reached for his cell and made an important call. The minute his boss answered, he didn't waste any time.

"You were right. He's holed up in an old warehouse. I saw her with his dog, but she's on foot now. You want us to follow her?"

Without hesitation, the stern voice of his powerful and connected employer gave him his orders.

"No. We can always take care of her later. He's the one I want. Kill the dog and bring him to me."

"We're on it."

He ended the call and reached into his glove compartment. The man kept his eyes on the street as he worked from muscle memory to fasten a suppressor onto his Glock and place the weapon on the seat next to him. After he turned the key in the ignition, he quietly drove the van down the alley. If he had to haul dead weight, he didn't want to break a sweat.

The mutt would be the first to go. He hated dogs.

Chapter 7

Downtown Denver

Minutes later

Mercer Broderick had forgotten what it meant to be civil to another human being. It had been awhile since he'd ever had to be. He sat in bed and quieted his dog, Karl, after his four-legged partner had reacted to his show of agitation. Karl would never have acted on impulse to attack Zoey, not without a command from him, but she didn't know that.

He hated seeing the hurt in her eyes. A woman's tears were the most formidable weapon known to mankind.

Zoey hid her vulnerability behind a false bravado. He found her bravery admirable. To run into a burning building took guts and she'd wrestled him to the ground without pause to save the life of a

86

friend—at great risk. But it was her willingness to bear her soul to a stranger that earned her his highest respect. Her honesty and her need to be loved broke his heart.

"We behaved poorly, but if it's any consolation, we did it for her sake." He stroked Karl's head and stared out the empty window. "She left just in time. It's not a very well-kept secret that we both could use a long bath."

Karl's ears perked at the word 'bath' and the dog cocked its head.

"Sorry, Karl. Nothing personal."

Mercer couldn't afford to feel badly for doing the right thing. In his world, playing by the rules or showing kindness could get him killed—or worse, someone else. Where he had to go, Zoey would want to come, but that would only get them both killed. He didn't need more ghosts plaguing his nightmares. He had more than his share.

It took effort to stand. When he tried to take his first step, his head spun and his eyesight blurred. The gunshot wound in his arm ached. Naked, Mercer headed toward the utility sink and washed up. After he grabbed fresh jeans and a T-shirt, he struggled to dress with only one good arm and the exertion wore him out. He would try the cold soup she'd brought for him, but not before he found his SIG Sauer P226.

Zoey had told him she put his gun somewhere safe. For a woman who ran into a burning building, he had no idea what her definition of 'safe' might be. Mercer searched his belongings and walked the perimeter of the room, looking for a likely hiding spot, but he came up empty.

When he heard a soft creak on the metal fire escape, he froze. His first thoughts turned to Zoey—thinking she'd returned—but Mercer didn't live a life where good things happened to him.

He gave Karl a silent hand command and crouched low with his eyes alert. Without his SIG, he'd have to improvise.

***

1:50 pm

Clive Barnwell eased up the metal stairs, keeping his back to the wall of the deserted warehouse. He had his partner, Frank Church, ahead of him. If anyone got shot, Frank made a bigger target. The way the guy farted, he wouldn't be missed. As Clive neared the open window, he gave a series of hand signals to Frank. The big man peered into the shadowy building and nodded. He gave the 'all clear' for Clive to follow him in and he'd cover.

When Clive hit the top landing, he glared into the open window. No sign of the dog or the man they'd expected to find. Frank skulked into the warehouse and covered for him with his weapon drawn, holding his gun in a two-handed grip. Clive crawled through the opening and stood beside his partner. He aimed his Glock into the dark corners as he shuffled across the floor in search of his target.

After Frank shrugged and furrowed his brow, Clive knew what that meant. Had he gotten the wrong warehouse? He'd paid two idiots to steal the girl's car and set off the alarm to draw her out. He'd watched from a distance and thought he'd gotten the right fire escape and window.

Clive gave another hand signal. He ordered Frank to split up to cover more ground. He headed for the mattress on the floor and what looked like personal belongings stuffed in a duffle bag. He sent Frank to check the trash and the utility sink. If this shit hole was occupied, he'd know soon.

"I got blood over here." Clive dared to speak up. "On the bed sheets."

"Bloody bandages in the trash and in the sink," Frank said. "He's lost a lot of blood. Maybe he went to a doc."

"Guys like him don't do doctors. No, she helped him." Clive lowered his weapon. "Who knows what he told her. I guarantee the boss won't like it. He'll want her dead. I'm making the call."

Clive reached into his jacket and retrieved his cell, but before he hit speed dial, he heard a bouncing thud and a low rumble of something rolling across the floor. He looked down at his feet and his brain had only one second to register what he saw.

A grenade.

"Holy Sh—"

***

After he deployed the flashbang stun grenade, Mercer turned his head and covered Karl's eyes and ears with his body. In protecting his dog, he would suffer some of the effects of the detonation. His hearing wouldn't be worth a damn, but he had to shield the only partner he had.

The blast was deafening. Everything in Mercer's world muffled and his ears rang. The concussion from the explosion damaged his inner ear and destroyed his body's sense of balance. He faltered like a drunk, but he had to move fast. He had precious seconds before his advantage would be gone.

The intense flash blinded the two men. The brilliant light in a dark room inflicted ghost images on their eyes. Disoriented, they lost their balance with the powerful blast, as he had, and fell to the floor. Dust and debris rained down on them as they gagged for air.

The only one not affected by the grenade had four legs.

Mercer gave a hand signal to Karl and the dog raced for the men on the ground, with him stumbling close behind. He would only have six seconds before the men regained their senses. Coughing, he grabbed their weapons, hoisted his duffle bag over his shoulder with a painful wince, and headed for the fire escape.

When he looked over his shoulder, Karl had done his job.

The dog gave his indication alert sign by zeroing on a cell phone that had dropped to the floor. Mercer gave another hand signal and the dog retrieved the phone with his mouth and brought it to him.

Let's go, boy. He only heard the muffled sound of his voice as he followed Karl out the window and down the fire escape. His injured arm grew numb and he ached with every step down the metal stairs as he lugged his duffle. Mercer had to put distance between him and the men who'd come to kill him.

After he hit asphalt, a florist truck sped down the alley, heading straight for him until it screeched to a stop. He pulled a gun from the waistband of his jeans—the suppressed Glock—and aimed it at the driver.

Zoey Meager sat behind the wheel with a stern look in her eyes and yelled out the open driver's window.

"Don't argue. Get in."

Chapter 8

Downtown Denver

2:15 pm

"You look rough." Zoey gripped the wheel and made a turn as her gaze drifted over his body. "How are you feeling? Did you eat before your world blew up?"

"Oddly, eating wasn't a priority. I'm afraid your soup didn't survive. Sorry." He truly was sorry and his stomach rumbled in a show of solidarity.

"We'll have to rectify that," she said.

Mercer noticed Zoey didn't have a key in the ignition and electrical wires hung below the dashboard, with mismatched colors entwined together.

"At the risk of sounding ungrateful, how did you start the engine? You don't have a key." He glanced at her face as she drove and noticed that she blushed.

"This isn't your car, is it?" he asked. "You're a car thief."

He had no doubt she'd hotwired the vehicle.

"I'm afraid that comes from my misspent youth in foster care. A kid can learn all sorts of interesting things under the watchful eye of the government." She kept her gaze focused on the road. "Where are you taking me?"

"Oh, no. You're dropping me off. The next corner will do."

"You look dead on your feet. Don't be silly."

"I don't *do* silly. I wouldn't know how."

"Oh, I bet if you put your mind to it, you could master the concept. Who were those men?"

Mercer didn't answer at first. He had too much on his mind with a clock ticking, but a woman like Zoey wouldn't settle for silence.

"I've never seen them before." He lied. "They weren't the welcome wagon."

"Who brought the explosive to the party? Was that you?"

"I wanted to make an impression."

She shot him a sideways glance with an expression he found hard to read.

"At the risk of giving you an opening," she said. "You need to tell me where to go."

"My pleasure."

Mercer had another stash of clothes, food, water, false IDs and weapons at another safe house, but with her to protect, perhaps he needed a veritable fortress. Under normal circumstances, he wouldn't let her near his secret locations, but nothing about Zoey was normal.

The men who'd come to kill him, one of them threatened Zoey's life—and that changed everything.

'She helped him. I guarantee the boss won't like it. He'll want her dead.'

She had no idea that she had a target on her back because of him. Her relentless meddling, stubborn determination and her unflinching love for a friend had put the crosshairs on both of them. He gritted his teeth and stared out the window. His mind raced with what he should do. If he parted ways with her, she'd be a sitting duck without a clue her life was in danger. But if he told her that brutal men were coming for her, who knows what she'd do?

He needed more than business as usual.

The tick of a persistent time piece pounded in his head to the pulse of a fierce migraine. If Kaity wasn't already dead, Zoey's friend would not have a long shelf life. Her days and hours would be numbered, given what he knew of the crew behind the abductions. Zoey had been right to worry and take matters in her own hands.

He would've done the same if he had ever been given the chance. Her torment flooded him with painful memories he didn't want to exhume, but he had no choice.

"Change in plans. Take a right." He pointed. "At that next light."

Zoey smiled as if she'd won the lottery. The woman had no idea—he was no one's hero.

***

An hour later

"Pull into the parking lot of that restaurant, The Bent Fork Grill, and drive to the rear." Mr. January leaned forward in his seat and peered through the windshield, directing Zoey where to go. "Park next to that black Lincoln Navigator and don't kill the engine. We aren't staying."

She'd been to the Loveland restaurant before, which meant they were north of Denver, just off interstate 25. She'd been following the road signs as she drove, but he hadn't told her where they were going. She only knew they were heading north.

After she parked, a beefy guy dressed in jeans, cowboy boots, and a blue chambray shirt emerged from the Navigator and tossed Mr. January the keys to his vehicle and a piece of dark fabric. *What the hell?* She hadn't noticed him communicating to anyone, yet both men acted as if they'd done this exchange many times before.

"Wipe it down and torch it." Mr. January opened the rear door to the big SUV and let his dog jump inside.

Even the dog knew what to do.

"Will do, sir." Beefcake cowboy hopped into the stolen florist van and drove away without another word.

Sir? Zoey had no idea who or what Mr. January was. Not even the Denver police could locate a proper name. His record had been sealed and Detective Estefan Cruz had tried to warn her that he was dangerous.

When Mr. January approached her, carrying a piece of black fabric, the hairs on her neck stood on end. What the hell had she gotten herself into?

"What's that?" She pointed to what he held.

"Mandatory head gear from here. I apologize for the inconvenience, but I prefer you not see where we're going."

He handed her a black velvet hood to put over her head. When she hesitated, he explained.

"Look, I would've preferred that we part company here, but I overheard one of those men threaten your life. Because you helped me, they think you know too much."

"But I don't. I don't know anything. Should I know something?"

He rolled his eyes.

"Maybe you should tell me something," she said. "That way I can die for a legit reason."

Mr. January heaved a sigh.

"Do you trust me?" he asked.

She glared at him and wavered before she said, "Yes."

For the first time she'd known him, he smiled and almost took her breath away.

"*Yes?* You say I tried to kill you. I live like a homeless man. I'm armed and I blew up the third floor of a warehouse with two men inside and now I'm taking you to a secret location I don't want you to see." He shrugged. "You trust me? *Me?*"

"Well, actually it's your dog. I trust him."

He shrugged.

"Now you're making sense. Get in."

***

Laramie Mountains
North of Cheyenne, Wyoming
Two hours later

Zoey nodded off twice as she sat in the backseat, wearing the black hood. She'd given up trying to memorize road noise and sounds, like they did on TV cop shows. She had no idea how much time had passed, but her mind had grown numb with boredom.

Mr. January relished the silence.

He hadn't bound her hands behind her back. She could've lifted the hood at any time and cheated, but she chose not to. Instinct told her that he had more to lose than she did in abiding by the arrangement for the hoodie.

"You asked if I trusted *you*, but I have a feeling you're the one who has more at risk. Am I right?" Her attempt to engage him in conversation didn't score a grunt.

"That guy called you 'sir.' Why? Does he work for you?"

Still no answer.

"If you're not going to talk to me, can you turn on some music?" She didn't wait for his reply. "How much longer will it be? My bladder is asking."

As if in answer, the radio erupted with classical music. The volume was turned up loud enough to drown out her version of twenty questions. Under her velvet hoodie, Zoey winced and raised her voice.

"Ever hear of Kenny Chesney, Luke Bryan or Blake Shelton?" she asked. "Or that classic song, *'Mama get a hammer, there's a fly on daddy's head.'* Or *'If the phone don't ring, you'll know it's me.'*"

"Doesn't...ring." His deep masculine voice sounded good to her ears, like a scented and warm blanket fresh from a dryer.

"No, I'm sure it's 'don't.' Country music gets special dispensation for bad grammar. It's a thing, like on Twitter."

Who knew? It took poor grammar to get Mr. January to open his mouth. When Zoey sensed the Navigator slowing down, she raised her head.

"We there?"

"Close enough. You can take the hood off now. It'll be dark soon."

Zoey pulled the hood off her head and waited for her bleary eyesight to clear. When she could finally see straight, her jaw dropped and she gasped.

A fiery sunset speared its flickering rays through a dense stand of trees. Mammoth Ponderosa pines and birch trees, Aspens, and Cottonwoods dappled the hills. The forest surrounded the biggest house she had ever seen in real life—a sprawling architectural wonder, the estate fit into the hillside as if it were part of the lush landscape.

The modulated buildings with their flat, terraced rooflines had countless vistas to view the grounds—or provide higher elevations for a well-placed sniper to defend the property. Sections of the complex were dug into a mountain. The design reminded her of ancient Native American cliff dwellings.

"You better turn around and leave before we get arrested. How do you know these people? You don't expect me to pick the lock, do you?"

Mr. January raised an eyebrow and unleashed a double-shot of his annoyance as he drove through a stone archway with an impressive iron gate. He didn't stop at the manned guard station. A man dressed in black BDUs—looking like a SWAT team member—waved him through with a nod. The sentry held an assault rifle in his hands.

"It's a...damned fortress." she whispered, after she saw more uniformed men with dogs patrolling the grounds. "What *is* this place?"

"This is my home," he said.

Zoey forgot to breathe.

Chapter 9

Laramie Mountains

North of Cheyenne, Wyoming

Evening

Mercer Broderick pulled the Lincoln Navigator into one of the bays and lowered the garage door before he turned off the engine. He stepped out of the vehicle and opened the rear cargo hold to let Karl have his freedom.

When he reached for his duffel bag, a large hand intervened.

"I'll take that and put it in your room." Stetson Debenham, his number two man, yanked at the straps of the canvas bag and hoisted it over his shoulder with a grin. "Good to see you in one piece, *compadre.*"

"This is Zoey Meager. She's my guest for a few

days. I'll fill you in."

"That would be a good idea."

"It's a pleasure to meet you." Zoey put out her hand and Stetson shook it. "But I didn't catch your name."

"I didn't throw it, ma'am, but nice try. Good to meet you."

Shy by an inch of Mercer's six-foot five, the tall lanky Texan wore faded wranglers with rattle snake cowboy boots and a maroon and white A&M ball cap. The man was a die-hard Texas Aggie. He had a deep baritone voice that made him a hit with the ladies and an easy-going style that deceived most men into underestimating him.

"I'll take care of your four-legged *amigo*," Stetson said. "Come on, boy. I bet you could use a good pisser."

Mercer escorted his guest into the house through a series of secured doors with high-tech cameras that followed every move. Zoey ran fingers through her dark hair. As much as she wanted to keep her head down and avoid 'big brother' watching, she couldn't help but stare at the slick high-tech measures.

"In case you're wondering, I don't have cameras in *every* room," he said. "You will have your privacy here."

"Yeah, that's a load off my mind. I thought I'd have to get creative in the shower."

When Mercer entered the estate through the foyer, Nilah Rolstad waited for him with her hand out. He'd texted her before he arrived and knew what she wanted. Mercer handed over the cell phone he'd taken off the man at the warehouse. Nilah had the skills to do a complete analysis. With any luck, he would have locations to check out, with men who'd be higher up the food chain in the organization.

"Run a GPS history on this phone. I want to know every move the guy made, even if he took a dump."

"You got it." She smiled at Zoey and didn't bother with the pretense of an introduction. "Good night. I hope you enjoy your stay."

"Uh, yeah. What time is check out?"

Nilah grinned, but didn't stop. The petite blond wore her straight hair in a tight ponytail and had on tattered jeans, a purple hoodie, with black and white checkered Vans on her feet. She was his computer expert and white hat hacker. In short order, Mercer would have everything on the bastard who tried to kill him and Karl.

"How many people live here with you? Is this a cult? Should I stay away from the Kool-Aid?"

Mercer marveled at how Zoey's mind worked as he ushered her toward one of the guest rooms.

"I'm sure you'll want to freshen up. I took the liberty of arranging for a change of clothes. I hope everything fits."

He let her pass and Zoey walked into the room with her eyes wide, but she stopped him before he left.

"I have a name for you," she said. "I call you Mr. January, coldest month of the year."

He leaned against the doorjamb, fighting a smile.

"I guess I deserve that. Hell, I've been called worse."

"I get it, that I won't know your name or anyone else's here, but why all the secrecy if this is home turf?"

"House rules when we have a guest."

"Not even your dog's name?" she asked.

"He's part of the team." He forced a smile.

Mercer turned to leave her alone, but Zoey called out to him.

"I don't know how this will help Kaity. I feel her slipping away and all this seems like a distraction. I turned my back on her once. I can't do it again."

Her eyes watered and her voice trembled. He fought the urge to hold her in his arms, but he kept his distance for her sake.

"I haven't forgotten about your friend," he said. "I brought you here because you're in danger, otherwise we would've said our good-byes back in Denver."

"I don't get you. You seem like a compassionate man. I've seen it in your eyes. I don't think I'm wrong."

"Looks can be deceiving, Zoey. Dinner will be in an hour."

Mercer closed the door behind him to give her privacy—and block out the expectation and vulnerability in her eyes. If he couldn't find Kaity alive, he knew how Zoey would look at him then. He had no future with a good woman like her, or anyone else, yet he'd let her under his skin. He'd invited her to his home—to what should have been a sanctuary.

Nothing good could come of it.

What the hell is wrong with you?

***

Forty minutes later

Dressed in jeans and boots, a dress shirt with rolled up sleeves, and a vest, Mercer swiveled in a leather chair behind his desk in the darkened room. He listened to a woman's disembodied voice chastising him over the phone—a secured encrypted line he had in the War Room, an underground bunker command post. If his estate were attacked, he had enough provisions, weapons, communications, and back-up power to sustain him and his team.

The Danish woman on the line helped build the complex that he'd started. Eva Henriksen had invested in him and his vision of swift justice, unrestrained by jurisdictional or international borders. She had a network of high powered people of influence across the globe that would disavow him in public, yet secretly turn a blind eye to his vigilante ways. Mercer straddled a tenuous line between law enforcers and law breakers to do what police and Feds couldn't. At odds with both sides, he'd have a collective bull's eye on his back if the public knew.

"I hear you almost got yourself killed, and now you brought home a stray," the woman said, with her distinct Danish accent. "She could jeopardize everything we've worked for."

Fatigue robbed him of words. His wound ached and he needed sleep and something to eat.

"She's part of this, too. I believe the people I'm searching for have a friend of hers. It's just a hunch, but from everything she's told me, we could be hunting the same traffickers."

"So why do you need her?" the woman asked. "You've got everything you require. She can only get in the way, or worse, she could distract you."

"They would've killed her. She had a target on her back because she stuck her neck out for me. I couldn't leave her behind." He rubbed his temple to soothe a burgeoning headache. "I appreciate your concern, but mission ops are mine."

"I suppose that's your polite way of telling me to buzz off."

"I would never use those words."

"No, you're too much of a gentleman," she said. He heard the smile in her voice. "Get some rest. You sound exhausted. Sleep well, Mercer."

"Good night, Eva."

After he ended the call, he sprawled deeper into his chair and shut his eyes. He relished the silence of the bunker, but when he sensed a presence, he spoke without opening his eyes.

"I don't want to hear it, Keiko. She's here. She's staying until I say otherwise."

He slowly opened his eyes as his bodyguard specialist emerged from the shadows—an ethereal beauty with a soft-spoken, measured way of speaking. Keiko Kayakova was raised by her Japanese mother, but trained in martial arts, weapons and tactics by her Russian father who had wanted a son. She had the lithe body of a dancer with pale skin the color of flawless ivory. Her straight black hair—as shiny as a raven's wing—made a vivid contrast to her ice blue eyes, her father's gift.

"Take off your shirt." She crossed the room and knelt at his boots, carrying a bundle in her hands. "Your dressing needs changing."

He didn't move at first. Keiko often had an agenda not easily foreseen. Mercer kept his eyes on her and unbuttoned his shirt, one button at a time. When he winced after he tried shrugging out of his vest, Keiko helped him remove his shirt.

"I am indebted to your guest," she said. "She helped you when I could not. I will care for her like I would my dearest sister."

"You were an only child."

"Don't wield facts against me like a weapon. You

should be grateful I am in a generous mood."

Mercer gritted his teeth while Keiko worked on him. Despite her outward appearance, she was not a delicate flower. Sometimes she inflicted pain simply because she could.

***

Keiko had been rougher on Mercer than she'd wanted to be. Why couldn't she be soft for him like other women? She disposed of his bloodied dressing and put away the medical supplies, but as she walked past the kitchen and saw Stetson making dinner, she knew it would be for Mercer and his guest—and she smiled.

"What's on the menu?" she asked.

She eased up behind Stetson and put her arms around his waist, hugging his back. She loved the hardness of his body and his dominating height. He reminded her of Mercer. If she couldn't have what her heart desired, Stetson made a satisfying physical surrogate.

"Red meat night. I'm grilling." He turned to hold her. "Are you hungry? Can I get you anything?"

"We don't have time for what *I'm* hungry for."

She smiled and ran her fingertips down his chest, playing with his buttons. In her mind she pictured Mercer in her embrace, but he had rejected her advances more than once. When he needed a woman to share his pain, he did not choose her. Mercer had assumed that she'd inherited her father's tough skin and she had, but when it came to the one man she wanted, Keiko turned to tofu.

"Let me finish dinner. You should help Nilah. I have a good feeling about that cell phone she's working on."

"Are you sure?" He kissed her cheek and she closed her eyes, pretending the lips on her skin weren't his.

"Yes. Now go, or dinner will be late," she said. "Get out of my kitchen."

She kissed him hard and he cupped his large hands on her ass and lifted her onto his hips to caress her in his strong arms. Now that Mercer was home— to serve as a constant reminder that she wasn't good enough for the one man she wanted more than life itself—she would need Stetson to satisfy her urges. She had plans to drain him dry.

When she was alone, to finish the menu Mercer had asked for, she decided to size up his guest. An overdose of hidden wasabi in a suitable appetizer might do the trick. There were many ways to inflict pain that were far more gratifying.

***

Mercer tapped on Zoey's closed bedroom door. When she didn't answer, he tried again. He knocked and said, "Zoey? I came to escort you to dinner."

Sounds came from inside the room, feet moving across wood floors and a low groan of frustration. Mercer leaned against a wall and crossed his arms, fighting to hide his amusement. When the door opened, Zoey had a sheepish smile on her face. She tried to block his view, but at his six-foot five height, she didn't stand a chance.

The clothes and shoes he'd furnished were strewn across her bed as if there'd been an explosion.

"I couldn't decide what to wear. It's a woman thing, mostly." She squeezed out the door and shut it behind her. "I could eat a horse. You ready to go?"

Mercer pursed his lips and didn't say a thing.

He followed Zoey down a hall and watched her move. She'd chosen a dress that looked great on her. It flounced in all the rights places for a man to

113

wonder what was underneath and her bare legs in sexy heels were tanned and shapely. Mercer would have to thank Ciara Flowers, his logistics and weapons expert, for her taste in clothes.

Mercer escorted Zoey to the formal dining room and at the entrance he waved a hand to let her pass. His team had overdone the ambience as if he were on a date, but he appreciated their effort. Lighting had been dimmed and candles flickered warmth across the room. A fire crackled in the stone hearth and a floor to ceiling window stretched across the breadth of the room and looked onto the expansive grounds.

"This is the most beautiful home I have ever—" Zoey stepped into the room, whispering, as if she were in a church.

"Can I get you some wine?"

"Yes, please, whatever you're having. I don't know much about wine, but in a room like this, I figured it's mandatory."

He poured two glasses of a fine Cabernet and handed her one, but before his guest took a sip, a door opened and Keiko rolled a cart into the dining room, making a show of her body. Mercer cringed.

"Dinner is served. Please have a seat." Keiko placed a small tray of sushi on the table, with soy sauce, pickled ginger and wasabi. "We start with my personal favorites."

Mercer knew from the look on Zoey's face that she wasn't a fan of raw food. He'd expected steaks, but Keiko had other plans.

"Please serve the main course," he said. "Then we would like privacy. Thank you."

"But sushi is brain food." She shifted her gaze to Zoey and said, "You could benefit from it."

Mercer glared at Keiko's obvious ploy to mess with his guest's head.

"In Mexico, they have a special word for sushi," Zoey said. "They call it...bait."

The Japanese woman shrugged and rolled her eyes, but when she opened her mouth for round two, Mercer shot her a look that put an end to her game.

Keiko left the room, but came back shortly with two sizzling ribeyes, baked potatoes, and asparagus spears. She did not normally cook or serve food to anyone. Others on his team were handier in the kitchen. It was a shared duty and he had a rotation, too. But Keiko had picked her spot to toy with Zoey. As long as he shared his home with his guest, Mercer knew he hadn't seen the end of Keiko's antics.

Zoey cut into her steak and sipped her wine, but

couldn't take her eyes off the heavily-treed property as she watched the last remnants of the day. The pastels of sunset and the soft flicker of candlelight played well on her skin and made him want to touch her. Zoey told him more about Kaity—the good memories—and she shared her life in the foster care system. She had an endearing way of telling a story that touched him. He loved the sound of her voice and the way she laughed.

But she unearthed bittersweet memories in him that hurt worse than being shot. He wasn't sure how he felt about a woman who stirred feelings in him that he thought were dead and wounds that never healed.

When they finished dinner, he went to the bar to refill their wine glasses, but Zoey had a look of agony in her eyes that he recognized, something he saw whenever she spoke of her friend.

"My instincts tell me you're a good guy," she said. "I know you want to help Kaity, but no offense, you don't love her like I do. She's the one person on this earth that I would do anything for."

Mercer fought the emotions Zoey had triggered in him. It was as if she'd seen through the labyrinth of walls he had erected to keep other people out of his life. Her compassion and fearlessness pierced straight through him and she held his heart in her hands.

"Sometimes love isn't enough," he said. "Sometimes it can be a weakness that clouds our judgment."

"No. I don't believe that. You brought me here because you wanted to protect me, but I can't stop thinking about Kaity. She's got nobody if she doesn't have me."

A tear slid down her cheek and glistened in candlelight.

"I'm here in complete luxury, having the best meal of my life with a mysterious and handsome man, but I feel like I've betrayed her." She reached for his hand. "I'm not doing enough. I haven't been able to sleep and I can't see my life without her in it, not when I can do something about it."

"I promise you, I can help. Give me a chance."

Her eyes welled with tears and she stared at him, without saying a word. Zoey said more with her eyes than she did with words. She broke his heart, but when Stetson Debenham barged into the dining room, he interrupted the moment.

"Sorry for the intrusion, but I need to borrow

your dinner companion, ma'am," he said to Zoey before he directed his gaze toward Mercer. "There's something you need to see, *jefe*."

Chapter 10

Laramie Mountains

War Room

9:10 p.m.

Mercer hated leaving Zoey alone on her first night in his home, especially as vulnerable as he'd seen her over dinner. Exhaustion and worry had taken their toll on her, but if she knew what he'd ditched her to do, she would approve and anxiously await news.

With any luck, the cell phone he'd given to Nilah Rolstad to analyze would reveal its secrets and give his team a target to focus on. He'd been working up the ladder of a shadowy and violent organization of human traffickers, working with his four-legged partner, Karl.

His team had assembled in the War Room, a below ground bunker and command center, located in the bowels of his home and accessible only by an elevator with an optical scanner. Keiko sat next to Stetson at a large conference table. Maddix McLeish, his high-tech security expert—the guy who had taken the stolen van off his hands—sat beside Ciara Flowers, his logistics and weapons expert and women's fashion diva. Karl had come with Ciara and arrived late to the party. He hopped onto a swivel chair next to his master, his reserved spot.

"Glad you got the memo, Karl," Mercer said. "Nice of you to join us."

The dog lowered his head and licked his junk.

"Now he's just showing off," Stetson muttered under his breath.

Without formality, Nilah held up a plastic bag with a phone in it and got down to business.

"The cell belonged to Clive Barnwell," she said. "I didn't get his ID off the phone, meaning I didn't have to hack into his service provider. That would be illegal and something I would never recommend."

"Half the things you do are illegal." Keiko raised an eyebrow.

"I like to think of it as half the things I do

are...legal."

"Set low standards and you'll never be disappointed." Keiko winked. "I get it. Words to live by."

Nilah ignored Keiko with a smirk. Mercer knew the women spent downtime together. Nilah had told him she thought of Keiko as a complex computer with one helluva firewall. She said there was never a barrier for the right hacker.

"I dusted the cell for fingerprints and scored a hit on AFIS to get ID. Clive has been a very bad boy. I made a copy of his criminal record for all of you. Peruse at your leisure."

Mercer flipped open the file she compiled from the Automated Fingerprint Identification System and glanced over other records he'd seen before when bad guys found criminal bosses with lucrative operations and pricey attorneys. Undercover, he'd observed Barnwell and his sidekick before, keeping bad company with other minor players, but he never had a name until now.

The man had started out with petty crimes as a teen until he stole a car and did time in Juvie. In the state's care, he learned real skills and hooked up with a network of low lives until he did his time and graduated into a thug for hire. He'd been implicated in burglaries, several fraud cases, an illegal gambling accusation, and ran hookers for his crew, but he'd become Mr. Teflon when it came to prosecution. Charges were dropped after evidence got lost or witnesses came down with a sudden case of amnesia.

Guys like Clive Barnwell were time bombs waiting to go off. Mercer wanted to stop him and the high-powered organizations that hired brainless muscle like him.

"Show us what you found when you back tracked his cell towers."

"My pleasure," Nilah said. "Will someone douse the lights? Thanks."

When the War Room went black, lit only by the dim glow of computer screen displays across the expanse, Nilah aimed a remote and hit a button. A holographic map projected onto a large panel. Laser points in red showed the cell towers that Barnwell's phone had pinged.

The colorful mass of dots looked chaotic to the untrained eye, but Nilah knew how to sift through the noise. Mercer had seen her make sense of highly complex cyber security firewalls, but when she unraveled a knot of Christmas lights, that's when he knew she had a true gift for deciphering insurmountable puzzles.

"Here we have a picture of his movement, en masse, over the last month," she said. "It looks like a jumble, until I dug into the details and narrowed down the specific locations he frequented."

Nilah explained how cell towers could only triangulate the physical location of a phone if Barnwell was on the move. That would limit his location to a general area, but Nilah had other ways to look at the data.

"For example, when Barnwell stopped into restaurants that had WiFi or he hit any identifiable mobile hotspots, I knew exactly where he was. The man is a creature of habit. As Mercer suggested, I can actually tell where he takes his morning dumps."

Keiko winced and when Stetson snorted a laugh, Karl cocked his head.

"I stripped out the places I identified as unessential." She shrugged. "A girl's got to start somewhere."

She pointed the remote to the wall panel and the holographic image changed. Half the chaotic network vanished.

"I cleared Clive's typical day from the map. Let

me tell you, he has a thing for a certain hooker, but hey, I'm not judging." She raised both hands and grinned. "I only made a note of her name in your files, in case you need to locate him. You can set your clock by that old horn dog. He's a straight up nooner."

Nilah hit the button again and changed the map. Once the map became simpler, it piqued Mercer's interest.

"What's Barnwell doing in Cheyenne?" He sat upright in his chair. "I thought he operated in the Denver area."

"Now that's a good question." Nilah grinned. "I couldn't pinpoint specific locations, so I had to resort to property tax records and other tricks up my sleeve. It seems Clive Barnwell visited some interesting places and people while he was in Wyoming."

Nilah handed him another file, before she shared it with the team. She wanted him to see it first.

"What are these? Satellite images?" he asked. "How did you get them?"

"I have my ways," she said. "It's probably best you don't know, but those are thermal images that show body heat. I believe there are hostages at that location. Here's the video where I downloaded the still shots. You'll see what I mean."

She punched the remote and eerie images of human shapes, wavering in colors that flared from green to red, moved in and out of a chamber where bodies were huddled. He could only guess what was happening, but the clustered people appeared to be hostages.

"If we can get close enough, it would be worth investigating, but that's your call." She handed files to the team.

"We need more intel, but this could be the break we've been looking for." Mercer couldn't take his eyes off the satellite footage. He couldn't help but wonder if one of the infrared bodies was Zoey's friend.

What he contemplated for his team was a domestic op that could finally bring down the large ring of traffickers he'd been hunting—without being encumbered by the law.

Most people were of the opinion that the word 'vigilante' had a distasteful ring to it. Vigilantes were perceived to be borderline criminals, walking a fine line between enforcing the law and breaking it. Mercer didn't care about people who would rather respect the rights of criminals over the rights of the victims. He'd learned the hard way that justice wasn't a given fact or a right unless he took matters into his own hands and controlled the outcome.

In a past life, he had been a successful CIA operative. At one point his job defined him, but not anymore—and not ever again. He'd discovered that 'drawing outside the lines' got better results. Rules were meant to be broken when they got in the way of true justice for innocent victims like Kaity Boyer.

"We're getting close. I can feel it." Mercer didn't realize he had spoken aloud until his team turned toward him.

"Why do you think this is them?" Keiko asked. "This could be only another tentacle of the octopus."

Mercer had been hunting a faceless network of cagey criminals. He'd heard only rumors of the existence of a covert organization of human traffickers—called the Hive. They existed online through a massive network of computers, flash drives, SIM cards, or anything electronic. Like shifting sand, they were completely adaptable and elusive.

Mercer had been on the street for weeks, with his ear to the ground in gang territory. Gangs were the lowest rung in the ladder. Every crew had a boss who had a boss. One by one, he and Karl tracked down the organization through links in Cyberspace.

Karl had a special skill.

"We won't know for sure until we get Karl inside."

His dog had been trained to detect the smell of computers and microchips. In the K-9 world of handlers and trainers, Karl was called a 'porn dog.' Mercer didn't know such an animal existed until a high-profile case involved a dog with Karl's skill set.

A TV personality, known for his endorsement of sub sandwiches, had eluded prosecution until a porn dog sniffed out his SIM card stash of child pornography. The tiny memory cards, used for storage in cell phones, had been easy to hide from two-legged law enforcement.

Who knew it would only take two more legs to break the case?

"We'll need a team on this. Complete surveillance before we move in. We have to get this right. Our bigger objective is to cut the head off the snake, but if we find evidence of hostages, their lives come first."

"You would risk our investigation for a handful of hostages?" Keiko asked. "What we do, sometimes there is collateral damage and people die, but if we can kill the snake, shouldn't that be our goal?"

He'd had this discussion with her before. There was logic in her argument to look at the bigger picture. It took a cool operative to think the way Keiko did, but not all missions fit her view of the world.

"I understand what you're saying," he said. "If lives weren't on the line, I might agree with you about focusing on the larger objective, but I will never sacrifice an innocent life for the sake of an op. Never."

Keiko nodded and didn't argue.

While his team talked strategy as they looked over the satellite imagery and video footage, Mercer thought of Zoey and what she'd told him over dinner. How much would he tell her? She would ask about the cell phone, knowing he had ordered the device analyzed for GPS coordinates.

It was only a matter of time before she would resent being kept out of the loop over 'need to know.' Or she might get feisty mad when she finally realized that he intended to keep her safe at his home, whether she wanted the protection or not. She would feel like a prisoner and he couldn't blame her. With Kaity missing and no leads on her disappearance, it tore Zoey to pieces.

She needed hope and he wanted to be the man to give it to her, but until his team did a full recon, he wouldn't know what they had, if anything. He felt an obligation to the victims held by the trafficking ring—countless destroyed lives—and he had a duty to stop the atrocities from happening to anyone else. He couldn't afford to make decisions based on one life. In that regard, he and Keiko would agree, but that didn't stop him from worrying for Zoey.

'Sometimes love isn't enough.'

That's what he'd told her. She must've hated hearing him say it.

He didn't think she could take the disappointment if they hit another dead end without answers. Time could be a cruel and formidable enemy. The odds of finding Kaity alive worsened by the day. Mercer didn't regret protecting Zoey, but he feared they were both careening toward a fate neither of them wanted to face.

Mercer prayed he'd be wrong.

***

After midnight

Wearing only a short kimono of black silk, Keiko crept down the dimly lit hall, heading for a room she knew well. When she got to his bedroom, she didn't bother to knock. She slipped inside and closed the door behind her. The rumble of a shower came from the bathroom. Reflected in the mirror she saw his muscular tanned body under the hot stream of water. Soap suds from shampoo trailed down his back and disappeared into luscious mounds of flesh.

Keiko licked her lips and stepped through the door. The silk of the robe felt wicked against her naked skin and her arousal tightened her nipples. She imagined warm wet lips sucking on them, hard. Billows of shower steam flushed her skin with heat.

With his back turned, Stetson could be Mercer if she willed him to be so. A lump wedged in her throat whenever she thought of the only man who had denied her. Mercer had his reasons, but that didn't mean his rejection stung any less.

She never felt good enough for a man like him.

Keiko dropped her silk robe to the bathroom floor and opened the shower door. Stetson turned in alarm and grabbed her neck. He squeezed until he realized who had invaded his shower and let go, but the sudden violence turned her on. When she gazed down his body, she noticed his impressive erection bobbing for her attention.

"Is that for me?"

When he smiled, Keiko dropped to her knees, closed her eyes, and thought of Mercer.

Chapter 11

Laramie Mountains

North of Cheyenne, Wyoming

2:00 a.m.

In a fitful sleep, Mercer tossed and turned, traversing a line between twilight sleep and unconsciousness. In a persistent and lucid dream, he drifted through a dark room, not knowing if he was truly awake, walking from one shadow to the next. He sensed a presence with him and his immediate thought went to her. Mercer pictured Zoey's sweet face and she appeared to him and stood by his side. She wore the dress she had on at dinner. When he took her in his arms, he smelled her scented skin and felt the heat of her body.

"I need you," she whispered. "Make love to me."

The warmth of her breath touched the skin of his

neck and his body reacted. A rush of blood flowed to his penis and he stiffened under his jeans. Mercer pulled her tighter to his chest and plunged his tongue into her mouth, tasting her tender lips. His hands grasped the firmness of her breasts and her nipples hardened into nubs under her dress. She moaned as she moved her body against him until he thought he would lose it.

Mercer picked her up and carried her to his bed.

When he threw back the white billowing bed sheets to lay her down, the clothes they both had worn disappeared. In a blink, Zoey sat on the edge of his bed, naked before him with her lips trembling as she stared at his hard cock. Mercer cupped her face in both hands and kissed her long and deep. His erection stiffened when he felt the coolness of her hand stroking him.

"I want you, Zoey."

He didn't know if he'd said the words aloud, but she spread her legs and pulled him down on top of her. Engorged, Mercer pushed into her and she groaned—the low, throaty sound of her pleasure. He thrust into her velvet wetness and swelled to fill her. Zoey writhed under him and took him deep inside her. When his tongue found hers, he devoured her mouth as he shoved in and out of her body. He wanted to pleasure her forever, but something prickled his skin like spiders racing across his bare back.

"Oh my, God," Zoey gasped. "Who's that?"

Her voice jolted him to his senses. Mercer shifted his gaze and stared down at Zoey. Her eyes were wide as she pointed to a dark corner of his bedroom with her body trembling.

"What's wrong with you?" She glared at him, angry. "They're here because of you."

He didn't understand.

"Who's here?"

"Them?" She thrust an accusing finger across the room and he turned.

In undulating shadows, silhouettes moved in the dark. Faceless bodies eclipsed the moonlight shining through his windows. The eerie horde drifted closer to his bed, watching him. Mercer didn't have to see their faces to know who they were. His nightmares never let him forget.

He awoke to the sound of him screaming, "No!"

His bed sheets were soaked and his lungs heaved for air. He'd had hellish dreams before, but with Zoey playing such a vivid part—as if she were one of his faceless regrets—it felt like a dark premonition.

***

Laramie Mountains
Next morning - Dawn

"See that she gets breakfast and make sure she stays put," he said to Maddix McLeish as he stood in the garage. "Zoey has seen you before when you picked up the florist van. She should be okay."

Mercer had Nilah Rolstad staying behind to coordinate their communications from the bunker command post. Zoey would have another woman around. After Mercer loaded food and water for Karl in the back of the SUV, he gave a hand signal for the dog to jump into the vehicle and secured the cargo hold. Mercer climbed into the passenger side of the Lincoln Navigator with Stetson behind the wheel, keeping the door open to talk to McLeish.

"What should I tell her if she asks for you or gives me trouble about staying put?" McLeish asked. "Women don't cotton to being told what to do."

"Say I'll fill her in as soon as I return. Tell her I'm working a new lead." He didn't want to promise something he couldn't deliver or lie to her. "Nilah is a familiar face if Zoey would feel more comfortable with another woman."

"Who are you? And what have you done to Mercer?" Ciara Flowers laughed. "Since when have you become Mr. Sensitive?"

His logistics and weapons expert stood in the next garage stall, loading her gear into a Silver BMW X3.

"Be careful, Ciara. Our Mercer has a soft spot for that one." Keiko grinned from behind the wheel of the BMW SUV.

"She's been through a lot," he said. "I want—"

"You're digging a nice big hole with those two, Mercer." Stetson said. "No matter what you say, you're only giving them more ammunition, *amigo*."

He ignored the ribbing from his team and turned his attention back to McLeish.

"Just do the best you can. Nilah will know how to get in touch with me."

Stetson engaged the ignition and pulled out of the garage with Keiko and Ciara in the vehicle behind them. Mercer's gaze shifted to the right-side turn mirror as his eyes searched for any sign of Zoey in his home.

The nightmare he had last night still had its grips

on him. What if in his desire to protect Zoey, he had put her in greater danger? A flood of horrifying images punished him and his guilt rose like hot bile in his stomach. Mercer shut his eyes to stop the torture.

"Are you okay?" Stetson asked.

"Yeah, I will be."

He lied.

***

Cheyenne, Wyoming

An hour later

Mercer lay on his belly in the dirt, staring through high-tech binoculars from a ridge. The cold ground chilled his skin through his BDUs and his injured arm throbbed in pain, but he ignored his discomfort and remained focused on his objective— the construction site below.

From Nilah's advance recon, he learned that a new medical facility would be erected once the building was completed. She needed more time to dig through the labyrinth of corporations and blind trusts to determine who had money in the project— and who might know about any hostages. A state-of-the-art health complex made a good cover for the seedy operation of a human trafficking network, brazenly hidden in plain sight.

His team had deployed to their assigned locations. A major construction project sprawled beneath his position, bordered by a cyclone fence with trespassing signs posted. In the gray of morning, employees were starting to arrive. A temporary mobile office, with a light and shadows coming from a window, indicated someone moved inside.

Mercer had Stetson positioned at the main gate as lookout. Ciara and Keiko took up positions below him on the east and west side of the property. He kept Karl in the warmth of the Navigator with his bed and water. No sense in every member of his team being cold and miserable. If they had an opportunity to deploy him, Karl would be eager to do his job.

"I need bird's eye visuals. You copy, Wizard?" Mercer spoke to Nilah through his ear bud, using her op handle to request the latest satellite images. The rest of his team would hear her response.

"Copy, Wolf. On it."

Satellite thermal scanners allowed Nilah to estimate a body count in the building and give him the approximate location where hostages might be held. It would be a long shot to get definitive proof of women being held against their will, but with any luck, the substantiation would come.

"Outbuilding on northeast corner." Nilah reported back after receiving updated satellite visuals. "A baker's dozen inside, three watching the hen house. One outside, two in."

She observed thirteen inside with three guards, but that didn't mean all the hostages could be trusted. Mercer knew from experience that traffickers with more than a few victims would use 'bottoms' to operate atop the hierarchy of sex slaves. Bottoms would collect money from the girls, discipline them, and handle day-to-day business. They were victims themselves that had earned the trust of the trafficker who gave them privileges over the others.

His team couldn't afford to turn their backs on anyone, once they breached the building.

"Incoming." Stetson's voice came over Mercer's ear bud as his number two man described a truck turning through the gate and onto the property.

Come on. Unzip your fly. Show us what you got.

"Get the tag, Boots."

"Will do."

Mercer prayed the yellow panel truck carried

proof they had found a viable link to the Hive. Cheyenne, Wyoming made sense. It had I-25 running north and south through the middle of it. I-80 ran west and east, making a perfect cross-hair hub for traffickers to haul their human inventory through the western section of the United States.

"If this is a delivery, I want proof, Lotus." He ordered Keiko to get digital photos of any hostages to run through facial recognition software.

"You'll have it." Keiko's disembodied voice whispered in his ear.

The truck kicked up dust as it jostled through the construction zone. When it didn't slow down at the project manager's office, the one with the light shining through the window, Mercer's heart pounded, hard.

"This is it. Make it count."

He followed the truck through his binoculars until it stopped near the outbuilding in the northeast corner of the property, the location where Nilah had found thermal scans of bodies. The old warehouse had no windows and only one entrance, a metal door. It would make a challenging breach, but it could be done. His mind already worked on how they would execute their assault.

When the driver jumped out of the truck, he had a man with him who opened the cargo hold and waved a hand at someone inside the truck. Mercer forgot to breathe as he waited to see who would emerge.

Two women crawled from the vehicle and cowered from the men who shoved them. One of the women held a small dark-haired boy who didn't look older than twelve. Mercer's stomach clenched when he saw the kid.

"You getting this, Lotus?" Mercer asked Keiko as he peered through his binoculars.

"Yes."

He had his confirmation. After dark, when they could launch a stealth attack with better odds of succeeding on a rescue, he could deploy Karl over the premises and hunt down any cyber network link on the property. If this were the Hive, their operation would have a high-tech means of communicating on the human inventory when they bartered on the dark web. He knew from experience, and his gut instinct, that he would find the bread crumbs he desperately needed to locate the head of the snake.

But as the men were taking the two women and the boy to the warehouse, the driver pulled a guard aside and gestured back toward the three hostages. The guard ordered the women and boy to stop at the doorway to the storehouse. The two men laughed and shared a smoke.

Mercer didn't like it.

"This doesn't look good." Stetson's drawl came over his ear bud.

When the two men appeared to have struck an agreement, the trucker ambled over to the hostages and took his time looking them over. The guards cheered him on. He grabbed the boy by the neck and hauled him back toward the truck.

Mercer cursed under his breath.

The kid fought hard—kicking and crying—until the man had to grapple him off the ground and hoist him over his shoulder. He was too small to put up a fight. The woman who had held the boy tried to stop the man, but the guards kicked her inside and shut the door. The despicable coward took his prize to the back of his vehicle to sample the merchandize.

"I brought the fitty. What do you want me to do?" Ciara's voice cracked.

She had brought the Browning M2, a .50-caliber machine gun. She'd sent the message loud and clear to Mercer and the team. She wanted to annihilate these men where they stood.

Mercer gritted his teeth until they hurt. He breathed through his nose to stop from throwing up. His words to Keiko repeated in his head and made him sick.

'I will never sacrifice an innocent life for the sake of an op. Never.'

He struggled for an answer, but nothing better came.

"Too risky, Reaper. Stand down. We have the others to think about," Mercer's voice sounded like a stranger. He felt like a damned hypocrite.

The hostages in the warehouse would have armed guards willing to sacrifice them for the sake of the larger operation. They were expendable. If Mercer allowed his team to retaliate against the driver for what he was doing to that poor kid, others would die for his inability to control his rage. He'd be risking many lives to save one.

He fought the sting of tears and lost.

"If anyone can't stomach surveillance, I'll see you at home base in two."

They had what they came for, but two more hours would complete the recon phase. By the time they returned home, Nilah would have facial recognitions run and his team could set up a stealth strategy to rescue the hostages after nightfall.

What happened to the boy was a vile reminder of why he'd formed his team in the first place. No court system would give true justice to the victims of rapists and murderers. Victims were either dead or wounded with emotional scars they carried with them for life. Traffickers enslaved human beings to sell them into sex slavery, forced labor, or they harvested and sold their vital organs on the black market as if their lives meant nothing.

"If you're staying, Wolf, I'm in." Stetson was the first to speak up, but the rest followed without hesitation. "No one can stomach this, but we owe it to all of them to get it right."

Even after he gave his team permission to head to home base, none of them would leave. Not even after things grew worse. The guards stood outside the open cargo hold and watched the assault. When the driver was finished with the boy, the other men took their turns.

Mercer had no doubt. The boy's accusing eyes would find him in his dreams.

"I want their faces on digital, Lotus." He seethed. "All of them."

"Done," Keiko said. "I get the driver. Dibs."

Mercer couldn't think of a more fitting sentence than to unleash Keiko Kayakova on the driver's sorry ass.

Chapter 12

Laramie Mountains

North of Cheyenne, Wyoming

Hours later

Zoey hadn't seen Mr. January all day. He'd left two familiar faces behind, but since she didn't know their names, it felt as if she were held prisoner. She'd managed to choke down a slice of toast and hot tea for breakfast, but as the day wore on, every minute brought pure agony as she worried over another day without Kaity. She had a bad feeling and was powerless to do anything about it.

When she saw the black Lincoln Navigator and another SUV barreling up the long drive toward the estate at dusk, she prayed for news. She raced for the foyer entrance as Mr. January entered the premises with his crew. It shocked her to see them all dressed in black BDUs with thigh holsters and Kevlar vests, as if they were a SWAT tactical unit.

'Who are you?' she wanted to ask, but what came out of her mouth sounded harsher than she meant it.

"Where have you been?" She raised her voice in accusation. "I thought...well, you don't want to know what I thought." She crossed her arms to hold it together, failing miserably.

"Give us a minute of privacy. I'll be there shortly," Mr. January said to his people and pulled her by the hand into a room off the foyer that looked like a library. He shut the door behind them.

"Whatever you thought of me, I deserve it." Mr. January had a hard time looking her square in the eye. "I have to leave again and I can't take you with me."

Zoey grabbed his shirt and held tight as she stared into his eyes.

"Is this about Kaity?"

"I hope so, but I don't want to mislead you. That smart phone we picked up at the warehouse, it led us to a trafficking cell. They could be linked to the group I've been hunting."

"The group you've been hunting? Who are you? Why are you doing this?"

When he didn't answer, she let her heart race with the prospect of good news until she realized what he'd left out.

"Do you think these people have Kaity?" she asked.

He hesitated.

"I can't be sure, but we saw proof they're holding hostages against their will. Do you have a picture of your friend? I need to see it."

Zoey reached for her phone and thumbed through her photos. She showed him her favorite, the one with the two of them, together.

"That's Kaity."

He stared at the image as if he were committing her face to memory before he shook his head and handed the phone back to her.

"These men are oxygen thieves who don't deserve to live," he said. "They're vile animals. We have to stop them, tonight."

Mr. January clenched his jaw in anger.

"You saw something bad, didn't you?" She tugged at his shirt. When he didn't answer, she knew.

"Someone has Kaity. They're hurting her, I just know it." She cried and turned her back on him. "I know you're not responsible, but I don't know what to do. I have to find her."

He came up behind her and pulled her into his arms, whispering in her ear.

"I will find Kaity if it's the last thing I do. I promise you."

The warmth of his body and tenderness in his voice made her feel safe. She wanted to shut her eyes and listened to him whispering promises in her ear all night, but she couldn't let that happen. With tears in her eyes, she turned toward him—standing on tiptoe—and held his face in her hands.

"We both know you can't make that promise, but there's a special place in heaven for a good man like you, Mr. January."

Zoey didn't know much about the man she wanted to kiss more than breathe—not even his name—but she would damn well know how his lips tasted, even if she never kissed him again.

She pulled him into her arms and devoured his mouth, caressing his tongue with hers. He lifted her off the ground and cradled her against his hard body. With a low groan of ecstasy, she burrowed into his warmth. She wanted him, needed him, but her emotions were raw. She didn't know if her feelings for him were real or she needed his strength more.

"Stop," he said. "We can't do this."

To her surprise, Mr. January was the one to put on the brakes a split second before she did. Panting and disheveled, he lowered her to the floor and held her face in his hands as he rested his forehead on hers.

"Don't get me wrong. There's nothing I want more than to make love to you, Zoey Meager. You are a desirable woman, but you can do better than someone like me." He nuzzled her neck until her knees nearly buckled.

"Someone like you?" She gasped for air.

"Don't put too much stock in whatever you see in me. I'm broken. I'll never be whole."

She tried to argue with him, but he placed a finger to her lips and gazed into her eyes until the room faded to nothing—all she saw was him.

"I have too many sins to make up for. You deserve a man who'll need you like breathing, a guy you can look in his eyes to know how beautiful you are, every day."

"But you—"

She wanted him to know that she felt more like a woman in his eyes than she ever had in her life. Zoey had never met a man like him. He lived in seclusion.

Even when he had people in his life, he chose to be alone and he erected walls to isolate his heart. Yet she couldn't think of any man more deserving of love and happiness.

What had happened to him?

"God, I wish I could be that man for you, honey, but some sins don't earn you a second chance."

He brushed a strand of hair from her eyes and pulled from her arms. His face had turned into a blank canvas—unreadable and distant. When he walked out the study door, he didn't look back and Zoey never felt so lost.

***

Cheyenne, Wyoming
Midnight

Dressed in tactical gear, Mercer sat next to Stetson Debenham in a black unmarked Ford F-150 SuperCrew truck with the engine running. In the crew cab, Karl sat behind Mercer wearing his work harness and leash. He heard his dog whine and pant as he paced the rear seat, eager to get his paws on the ground.

Ciara and Keiko were in a panel van behind

them, a vehicle with enough room to rescue all the hostages. Both transports were parked within sight of the construction project's front gate.

"Are we a go, Wizard? Confirm with visuals." Mercer spoke into his com unit to Nilah.

He needed confirmation that the hostages were still in play where he expected to find them. Since the metal door posed a challenge, Ciara planned explosives to gain entry. Nilah knew to confirm the hostages would be positioned away from the blast.

"You have a go, Wolf. Targets confirmed and positioned toward rear."

Mercer used a night vision scope to do a final assessment of the outer perimeter before his team executed their raid.

"One on gate duty. Easy on the takedown."

An armed security guard in uniform was on duty at the entrance. Since Mercer had no way of knowing if the guard played a role in the trafficking ring, he ordered the man be spared.

"He's mine. Wait for my signal." Keiko's voice came over Mercer's ear bud.

From the corner of his eye, he saw her shadow move through the dark, heading for her target. Keiko created a sound diversion to draw the man from the guard shack. She dispatched him in seconds, rendering him unconscious and zip-tied him hands and feet before she opened the gate and gave her signal.

"Let's make an honest woman out of her. Hit it." Mercer gave the order for his team to move. "We're doing this blind. No lights."

Stetson hit the gas with Ciara close behind, both vehicles running without headlights. His truck barreled through the gate, jostling over ruts in the dirt and kicking up gravel. Keiko jumped into the van and Ciara punched it to catch up.

When Mercer saw the warehouse ahead, where the hostages were held, he had Stetson stop at a distance to see if guards were posted outside. He peered through his night vision scope.

"Can you give me a headcount on the opposition, Wizard? Inside and out."

Nilah's voice came over his com unit.

"Only one outside. Hard to read the others, but I see three moving freely inside."

"I'll take the one outside," Mercer told his team.

He gave Karl a hand signal to stand down and stay.

"Not yet, boy. Soon."

Mercer retrieved his Remington 700 sniper rifle from the bed of the truck, a .308 custom-made bolt action precision rifle with suppressor and a box magazine. He took a prone position and adjusted his scope to take the shot and chambered a round. When the guard stepped into his cross-hairs, he slowly let out his breath to still his body, slipped his finger onto the trigger and took the shot. His rifle bucked and spat and a faint muzzle flash pierced the darkness. The man dropped like a rock and went down without a sound.

A clean head shot.

"Reaper, you're up next."

Mercer had cleared the way for his team to breach the metal door, the last barrier before they rescued the hostages. The door breach and bangers would be the diversion they'd need to disorient the remaining guards.

The truck and the van eased up to the warehouse, making a defensive wall of their vehicles to give them cover if they needed it. With precision from the many hours of training, his team split up to do their jobs. Mercer and Stetson took positions near the only door.

"Check the lock."

Mercer had seen it before. A tactical team pulling out all the stops to annihilate a door when it wasn't locked. Training officers loved to pull the prank to teach rookies a lesson, but this wasn't training. Lives depended on flawless execution. When Stetson reached for the handle, it wouldn't budge. Locked.

"Breacher up."

Mercer called for Ciara to set up the explosives, strip shaped charges adhered to the door and positioned along the door hinges and lock to blast the door apart. An explosives breach ratcheted up the stakes for his team and for the victims inside—it jacked up his team's adrenaline and made everything more dangerous—but Ciara was the best and it was the quickest method to gain entry. Nilah had confirmed the hostages were positioned to the rear of the building with walls between them and the front door.

Ciara had prepped for the mission and had pre-cut lengths of shaped charges. She stuck the explosive strips to the door the way they agreed in their strategy planning.

"Take cover," she said.

Mercer and his team inserted ear protection and used the warehouse as a shield to protect them from the detonation. In seconds, a thundering blast erupted. Dirt and billows of smoke rode the wave of the concussive force. Mercer and his team didn't wait for the dust to settle.

"Go, go, go!" Mercer gave the order.

With bangers in hand, Stetson deployed two stun grenades and stepped through the door with his weapon aimed—an M4 carbine. The cowards inside didn't know what hit them. The stun grenades blinded them with a burst of light meant to give them ghost images on their eyes. The loud blast disturbed fluid in their ears and caused them to lose balance. The men groveled on the floor, disoriented and blinking back tears.

"Policía!" one of them screamed, covering his head.

A voice yelled from the back room.

"I'm torching the place."

"*Armas abajo.*" With rifle aimed, Mercer yelled commands in Spanish to the traffickers, unsure if they spoke English. "*Manos arriba.*"

"Weapons down, hands up." Stetson echoed his words in English and moved deeper into the outbuilding with his M4 aimed at the enemy. "Hey, Wolf. Aren't these the same bastards who assaulted that boy?"

As the smoke cleared, Mercer took a closer look and his anger flared.

"Yeah, that's them."

When Keiki came through the door, she recognized the men on the floor, too. She'd taken their photos and run them through facial recognition. If anyone knew the faces of the men who'd raped the boy—she did.

"Bastards!" she cursed.

Kieko opened fire and killed the men without hesitating. Two to the heart, she executed them.

After what they'd seen that morning, the atrocity between the truck driver and the innocent boy, Mercer knew emotions would run high with his team, but he hadn't expected Keiko to shoot. The men were no immediate threat, but Mercer didn't have time to question her decision to shoot the men.

"There's one more. Find him." Keiko cried out. "I smell gasoline."

Keiko was right. He smelled gas, too. The stench hadn't been there when they first came into the building. The missing man—they had to find him.

With the potential of an active shooter still on premises, Stetson took lead and threaded his team through the dust and debris, following the sounds of screaming and crying from a back room. He edged his back along a wall and peered into the room. Someone took a shot at Stetson's head and he ducked. A wood splinter cut his cheek and when blood trailed down his neck, he cursed under his breath.

He gave hand signals to Mercer, who nodded and took up his position. Mercer heaved a deep breath and slowly glanced into the dimly lit space.

The odor of gas came from the room.

It looked like a torture chamber. Chains with manacles hung in one corner. Blood stained the floor. A piss bucket sat in the open and reeked of urine and shit. On the other side were the hostages, huddled together and clutching blankets to their chests. An old stained mattress had been tossed along a wall. Mercer knew that's where the traffickers raped their victims, with a captive audience forced to watch in horror, knowing their own degradation would come.

Something else shook him—the empty gas can on the floor by the hostages.

"I'll shoot her. She don't mean nothin' to me. I'll do it."

A filthy sweaty man held a young girl, using her

as a shield. He had a gun to her head with his shaky fingers on the trigger.

"You smell the gasoline, cop? It's everywhere. One spark will set it off and they all fry," he said. "Make me a deal, Mr. Policeman. Let me walk out of here and she's yours."

Mercer had no doubt that the man holding the hostage had set the fire in Denver, the blaze that killed the three women he didn't know were being held in the locked storage unit. The Hive had been eliminating their unwanted inventory by arson and killing their victims in the worst way.

Now the little coward wanted a deal with police and Mercer let him believe what he wanted. He took advantage of the standoff by taking another peek into the room.

When he took a closer look at the woman hostage—from the shadows in the corridor where he stood—he realized that he stared into the crying face of Kaity Boyer and a rush of emotion wedged his throat tight.

Bruised and battered, the girl looked rail thin, like a refugee who'd been through hell in a war zone. She hadn't been kept in good condition, which meant she'd been used up and tossed back to the vermin who held her. When even they wouldn't have her, she'd be killed.

Mercer didn't have time to explain to his team. He fixed his eyes on Stetson and Ciara, conveying what he could without a word, before he lowered his M4 and raised his hands.

"I'm coming in. I'm unarmed. Don't shoot."

He had a Glock tucked into his belt at the small of his back, but he didn't know if he'd have time to reach for it. He trusted his team to back his play. Mercer stepped into the room and locked eyes with the man who held Kaity Boyer's life in his hands.

In seconds it would be over.

Chapter 13

Cheyenne, Wyoming

1:00 a.m.

With his hands raised, Mercer stared at the coward who manhandled Kaity Boyer and used her for a human shield.

"A friend of yours sent me, Kaity. She loves you very much."

The girl gasped and fresh tears streamed down her cheeks.

"I thought I'd never see her again."

He shifted his gaze back to the abductor.

"I need to see the others." Mercer pretended to be a cop with rights and the armed man let him search the room for the other hostages.

A huddled mass of terrified human beings cringed in a dark corner of the room. They clutched at each other and cried. Many were in shock. When Mercer found the small boy he'd seen earlier, he slowly nodded his head to the kid and his mother.

He made a silent vow he would die trying to free them.

"All of you, shut up." The man hoisted Kaity off the ground and she screamed. He shoved his gun into her head, hurting her. "Back off and let me go or she's dead."

Mercer inched closer and gave his team a clear shot at the man. If they understood what he meant for them to do, they would wait for the perfect moment to take their shot. Stetson and Ciara were his best marksmen, but he needed to give them an advantage.

"What's your name?" Mercer asked.

The man backed into a corner and kept looking over his shoulder. Mercer couldn't tell what had his attention and it bothered him.

"You don't need to know that." The guy jutted his head out from behind his hostage and sneered.

"I thought you'd want your name on your grave."

Anger replaced the smugness on the man's face and he moved back again.

"I'll shoot her." He spat. "Don't think I won't."

"If you do that, I'll have the time I need to break your neck. You won't have a shield anymore." He glared at the man and inched closer, with his voice ice cold. "I don't need a weapon to kill you. Do you believe me?"

"I'll torch the place. Stay back."

"No you won't. You'll be the first to sizzle. You're standing in gas, genius."

The man jerked his head and looked down at his feet. He stopped glaring at the door, expecting company. He stayed focused on Mercer and whatever had his attention behind him.

"Stop moving. Stay right there," he demanded. "You're just messin' with me."

"Tell me your name."

"Quit askin' me that. Let me think."

"Thinking isn't your strong suit. If you were thinking straight, you would let her go and join your friends in the other room. They're waiting for you. You could screw things up for them if you hurt her."

The man's eyes grew wide and he called out to his buddies.

"Russell. Arturo. Are you out there?" he shouted.

The more agitated he got, the more he became careless. The weight of the girl had taken its toll on his strength. She drooped in his arms and soon his team would have a clean shot.

"You'll have plenty of time to talk to them after you let the girl go. I promise." Mercer shifted his gaze to Kaity and stared until she stopped crying. "Make your play, little man. Or I will."

When Mercer made his threat, the man had enough of his menacing taunts. He shifted his weapon toward him and took aim, letting Kaity drop to the floor.

"Say goodnight, cop."

Mercer went for the gun at his back. But before the man pulled the trigger, Stetson and Ciara raced through the door with guns blazing. Bullets pummeled the body of the last trafficker. He stood and took every shot. The man was dead before he hit the ground.

Mercer raced for Kaity and picked her off the floor, holding her in his arms to shield her. Stetson, Ciara and Keiko swept the room with weapons drawn. It was over.

Winded, Mercer clung to Kaity and let her cry. He whispered in her ear that she was safe. She'd get help and be home soon, but when he turned his back on the other hostages, a woman's angry scream forced him to turn around.

One of the hostages had a gun and she took deadly aim at Mercer—and pulled the trigger.

Chapter 14

Cheyenne, Wyoming

1:40 a.m.

Mercer only had time to think of the girl crying in his arms. The second the armed hostage pulled the trigger, the gun blasted and he turned his body to shield Kaity. More gunfire erupted. He waited for the punch of a bullet to strike him. When that didn't happen, he slowly turned to face Keiko.

She stood in front of him with her eyes wide—in shock and gasping for air. For the first time, he saw fear in her eyes as she fell into his arms.

"What happened? Are you shot?" He lowered Keiko to the floor, not taking his eyes off her.

"She stepped in front of the bullet." Ciara rushed to his side and knelt next to Keiko. "I had to take out the hostage. I had no choice."

The woman with the gun must've been a 'bottom,' one of the hostages that the traffickers had in charge of the others. That's why the man who held Kaity had nervously glanced over his shoulder, knowing she had a gun to back him up.

Keiko panted for air and reached for him.

"Where are you shot?" he asked. "Why did you do it? You didn't have to—"

"Early Christmas present." She coughed and her face grimaced in pain. "I can't breathe. Help me take this off."

She tugged at her body armor and Mercer helped her with the Velcro straps. Her lungs filled with air when he took the vest off and she rolled to one side.

"Any holes?" She glanced over her shoulder, twisting her body, and ran fingers over her back to search for bullet wounds.

Mercer saw a large hematoma the size of a softball, along her ribs and spine. The vest stopped the bullet, but the impact gave her a huge blood bruise. She'd be feeling the pain for days. When her eyes met his, Mercer cupped her face in his hands.

"Don't ever do that again," he said. "Not for me."

Her eyes welled with tears, but she only nodded and said, "Help me up, tough guy."

Keiko hadn't thought. She'd reacted on selfless instinct to protect him, knowing she might die. No one stepped in front of a bullet without understanding the consequences. His bodyguard specialist took a bullet for him—something she'd been trained to do—but from the look in her eyes, he wondered if Keiko had done it for another reason.

Mercer helped Keiko stand and ran a finger down her cheek, mouthing the words, "Thank you," before he faced his team and the hostages.

"Let's get these people to safety," he said to his crew before he spoke to the women and boy. "*Está seguro. Siga este hombre.*"

He told them they were safe and the women cried and clung to each other. He asked them to follow Stetson. His man went to the boy who'd been assaulted and cradled the kid in his arms, escorting him and his mother to the van.

Mercer would have the hostages checked at a nearby hospital. He would arrange to have their medical bills paid and support their long term recovery by offering counseling for those who wanted it. It wouldn't be enough for the horror they had survived. The road to recovery would be lonely and long—a lifetime—but he vowed to do what he could.

When he turned to Kaity, she collapsed in his arms and broke down. She could barely stand.

"Shh. You're safe now," he whispered in her ear. "Zoey never stopped looking for you. She loves you so much."

He repeated the words in a soothing voice until she went limp in his arms. Mercer lifted her off the floor and carried her to the van, covering her eyes so she wouldn't see the dead men.

After they loaded up the survivors, Mercer ordered his team to take them to the hospital, but he and Karl wouldn't join them until later—Karl had work to do.

Mercer prayed they would find the head of the snake this time.

***

Laramie Mountains
North of Cheyenne, Wyoming
1:50 a.m.

Zoey paced the floor in the library, the room where she'd kissed Mr. January. She felt closer to him there. She stared out the window onto the pristine grounds. Security lights cast eerie shadows on the trees and every dark hollow looked as if it moved under the moonlight and the sway of branches.

When a woman barged into the study, looking anxious with a sense of urgency, Zoey startled with the intrusion.

"I need you to come with me. Now," the woman said.

"Where are we going? Does Mr. January know?"

"Mr. January?" The woman smiled. "Does he know you call him that?"

"Yes, I told him." Zoey raised her chin in defiance. "He said he'd been called worse."

"Well, ain't that the truth." She grinned, but when Zoey didn't budge, she said, "Mr. January found your friend. She's alive. He's taking her to a hospital. He wants you to meet her there."

Zoey couldn't help it. The news felt like a gut punch, the very best kind. She broke down and didn't care who saw. Tears flooded her eyes and she dropped to her knees, crying and praying.

"Oh my, God." She clutched at her stomach and doubled over. "I didn't think I'd ever—"

"You're very lucky. We're very lucky." The woman corrected herself. "We don't always get good news on abduction cases. Come on. Let's go."

This time, Zoey didn't hesitate. She got to her feet and followed the woman Mr. January had sent to her. She'd get a chance to thank him, face-to-face, and it warmed her heart.

***

Cheyenne, Wyoming
2:10 a.m.

Wearing gloves, Mercer broke into the project manager's office in the construction zone, using a lock pick. He had Karl harnessed and on leash until they got inside. The dog paced with excitement and wagged his tail, anxious to work. Inside, the office was dark until Mercer flipped the lights.

A desk had a computer hard drive, as well as a laptop. He would confiscate those, but he let Karl off leash and put his partner to work.

"Seek." He gave the command and the dog lowered his head and swept through the space, darting back and forth until he gave his indication sign—laying down and whimpering.

Mercer knew he'd struck gold when Karl yelped at a wood panel wall behind the desk. He narrowed his eyes, unsure what the dog had found. Nothing was obvious.

"What is it, boy?"

Mercer used his hands to run along the wall. He knocked and noticed a hollow sound and cooler air wafting in from along a seam. Seconds later, he found a secret compartment and punched it open. Karl nudged his nose inside and licked his big score.

"Good boy." He gave Karl a treat after he found a thumb drive and a SIM card locked in a plastic case. "Bingo."

He couldn't imagine a good legitimate reason for a construction site to use a secret compartment to hide electronic media or storage devices. Only criminals used such things.

"You're brilliant, Karl. Nilah will be very happy."

He retrieved the devices, careful not to ruin any fingerprints, and dropped them into a plastic evidence bag. As if she were a mind reader, Nilah's voice came over his com unit. She sounded excited. Her energy came through his ear piece.

"I'm heading to Cheyenne Regional Medical Center, West. I should be there in thirty minutes. I've got Zoey with me. Where are you?"

Mercer kept his full attention on Karl.

"Seek." He gave another command to his dog

and had him work the other side of the project manager's office.

"We're almost done," he said. "Karl is still working. Give me twenty minutes and we'll be gone. You can make that anonymous call to report bodies at the construction site. Let the project manager explain why traffickers are using his location to cover their illegal operation."

"Will do, but I thought you might want to be at the hospital when Zoey sees Kaity. That's why I called, to give you a heads up to meet us. You deserve to be there, Wolf."

"Let me think about it."

Mercer shut his eyes and took a deep breath. To see Zoey happy would give a lift to his soul and he could use it, but she didn't need him around to get back to her life. He'd only be a reminder of what happened. Zoey would have her best friend, a survival story that rarely ended well, and he would have his mission with Karl. That had always been enough.

"Oh, come on. You know you want to see this." Nilah pleaded. "We don't get good news often. Come be with your team. Take a victory lap."

"Thanks for thinking of me, Wizard."

"That's the spirit. See you there."

"Come on, Karl. Let's go, boy."

After his dog gave his last indication and an iPad had been retrieved, Mercer loaded his four-legged partner into the Lincoln Navigator and climbed behind the wheel. Nilah would have plenty to analyze. Bit by bit, he had torn at the structure of the Hive, degrading its foundation in search of the head of the snake. He hoped to give Nilah another piece to the puzzle. Whether that happened or not, the mission had been a success for the lives they saved.

Mercer turned on the SUV engine and headed for the construction site front gate. He imagined Zoey seeing Kaity for the first time and he smiled.

With his hands on the wheel and the engine running, he stared at the road with a decision to make. Left, he'd see Zoey at the hospital. Right, he would go home. Zoey had never made anything easy on him. Why would tonight be any different?

Mercer made his turn—and his choice.

***

Cheyenne Regional Medical Center, West

2:45 a.m.

Zoey had ridden in the back of a windowless van, unable to see her departure from Mr. January's fortress. The woman with no name had driven her. She'd smiled and seemed nice, but the woman didn't speak during the trip, and she wouldn't answer any of the thousand questions Zoey had racing through her mind.

But that didn't matter.

Zoey would soon see Kaity. She cried every time she pictured her friend's face. It made her sad to think she'd eventually have to apologize for what she had done, and confess everything, but for now she only wanted to hold her and take care of her—because that's what sisters did.

When the van slowed, after a journey that seemed to last forever, Zoey thought she'd throw up. Every cell in her body splintered into countless nerve endings, all on fire. As the van door opened and the woman greeted her, she raised a hand to stop Zoey from bolting from the vehicle.

"You're at Cheyenne Regional Medical Center, West. She's in the ER, through these doors and to your right. When you see a familiar face, he'll tell you where she is."

Zoey jumped from the van and shot through the automated doors of the emergency room entrance. She looked for the face of Mr. January. He did exactly what he'd promised he would do—he found Kaity.

With her heart on full throttle and her lungs heaving, she saw him standing with his back to her in the corridor outside an intake room. His broad muscular shoulders looked good in his tactical gear. The kiss they shared flooded her mind and the warmth of his arms filled her. She didn't slow down until she grabbed his sleeve and spun him around. She wanted to thank Mr. January.

"You did it. You found her. Where is she?" she asked. "Where's Kaity?"

She felt dizzy from the blood rush, but the sight of him jarred her.

"You're not Mr. January? Where is he? I expected to—"

The tall man dressed in black BDUs gave her a lazy smile. She'd seen him before.

"No, ma'am." He drawled. "I'm not *el jefe*, but you have someone very special waiting to see you...right through that door."

Shaking all over, Zoey reached for the door and pushed it open. The sight of Kaity shocked her. She looked so very small in the hospital bed. Her body had shrunk and she'd been beaten. Bruises covered her face and arms and her eyes didn't have the same light behind them. When Zoey forced words from her mouth, she said the only thing that came to her.

"You're beautiful. I love you so much."

She slowly stepped toward the bed and cradled Kaity in her arms. She never wanted to let go.

Chapter 15

Laramie, Wyoming
A day later
Midnight

Keiko Kayakova had inherited her enduring patience and her steadfast discipline from her Japanese mother. Those qualities served her well over the years. She meditated daily and found reflective solace in the meticulous care of a Bonsai tree, one of her favorite pastimes.

She cared for a Japanese Shimpaku with its exquisitely textured bark and soft mounded juniper needles that she'd inherited upon her mother's passing. Her mother had acquired the rare specimen from the Ishizuchi mountain range on Shikoku Island, an uncommon beauty indeed.

Keiko thought of her Bonsai as she pulled her Harley-Davidson Dyna Low Rider motorcycle into the Laramie View Inn off I-80. She found a discreet spot to park, turned off her engine, and took off her custom helmet with dark tinted face shield and left it hanging off a handlebar.

She hadn't planned to stay long.

Keiko spied the vehicle she'd been following, parked in front of room 102 on the ground level. The seedy motel didn't have many patrons, except for the few who rented rooms by the hour. She walked up to 102 and knocked twice. When a man opened the door—five-foot ten-inches, dark hair and eyes, a knife scar on his cheek, and a beer belly—he took his time ogling her body before he said anything.

"Do I know you?"

"No. Do you care if I have a name?" she asked and didn't expect an answer. "The front desk thought you might want company."

"Come on in." The man shrugged and sneered. "Take off those leathers and I'll give you something to ride, slant."

She took her time and sauntered into the room with her leather chaps swishing. The only way out would be the way she'd come in.

"What are you lookin' for, chink?"

"I'm not Chinese."

"Do I look like I care? Pussy and ass push the same, darlin,' but hey." He narrowed his eyes at her. "Where did you get those blue eyes, slut? Your whore momma spread 'em for the white boys? Like momma, like baby girl."

His insults rolled off her like water. She thought of her Bonsai tree and how a delicate stream of water sluiced off its branches to nourish the plant's roots.

"Shed them clothes and get down on your knees, bitch. How much for a tune up?"

"Do I look like an *a la carte* menu?"

She gave him a price, knowing he couldn't afford it, but he surprised her. It must've been payday.

"For that kind of money, you're staying until I say I'm done." He opened his wallet and put bills on a nightstand. "And you don't say no to anything."

"The same goes for you."

He laughed until he noticed she wasn't smiling.

"I said strip, bitch. Now."

Keiko unzipped her black leather jacket and opened her arms wide—an invitation.

"I heard you like it rough," she taunted. "Come make me."

The man stepped close enough for her to smell the stench of his breath. He expected her to back into a corner, but Keiko had other plans.

She reached for the Japanese fighting knife she had sewn into the sleeve lining of her jacket—the blade had been a gift from her Russian father. Before the man blinked, she had sliced two large gashes across his chest. His skin splayed open and blood gushed from the wounds. When she twisted her wrist, she came down and across with the blade. She cut through his belly, deep enough to see his intestines spill into his hands.

"For the boy you raped yesterday."

The man stared down at his mortal wounds in shock, flapping his lips for air like a dying fish.

"What did you—?"

He dropped to his knees, crying like the kid he'd violated.

Keiko didn't say a word. She went to his bathroom and grabbed the plastic liner from his ice bucket. When she returned to the man, she held the bag under his belly and let his blood fill it as if she were milking a cow.

"W-What are you d-doing?" He slurred his words and his eyes drooped as he held his guts in.

"Your death will serve a vital purpose. You will nourish my Bonsai."

The blood of Keiko's enemies kept her venerated mother's Bonsai strong.

As the man died, writhing on a bloody carpet in a cheap motel room, Keiko cleaned off her jacket and chaps and straightened her hair in the bathroom mirror. Leaving the money on the nightstand, she stepped over his body and carried the bag of blood to her motorcycle.

She loved a night ride.

***

Laramie Mountains
North of Cheyenne, Wyoming
Two days later - morning

The confiscated thumb drive, SIM card, and other evidence of criminal activity that Karl had found at the construction site had set Mercer on a different path to hunt the Hive. New associations were charted and the next level of the organization would soon shed light on how the network operated and bartered in human flesh on the dark web.

Nilah made sure to secure back door access to the online network before the organization became aware of the construction office break in. As predicted, the Hive had shut down its old portals and logins, but not before Nilah had slipped her hand into their cookie jar for future access.

Today Mercer worked alongside Nilah in the bunker command post. They hunkered down at the conference table and poured over the downloaded data displayed on the holographic panel. Nilah had peeled back the layers Mercer would need to attack the Hive where it would hurt the enemy the most. He and Nilah were establishing their next strategy and finalizing a game plan to be shared with the team within the next few days.

Despite their last successful raid, his computer expert had been disappointed—in him.

"You should have been at the hospital," Nilah said. "I could tell Zoey was upset you weren't there."

"I bet she's already over it." He kept his eyes down as he wrote something down on a notepad. "She doesn't need a guy like me."

Nilah reached for his hand to stop him from writing and squeezed his fingers.

"A guy like you? Any woman would love a man like you. Don't give me that bullshit." She stared into his eyes and didn't flinch. "The only reason I'm bringing this up now is because Zoey is taking Kaity home tomorrow. If you leave now, you'd have time to talk to her in Cheyenne before she goes back to Denver."

Mercer cocked his head.

"How would you know this?" he asked. "Did you bribe someone at the hospital to spy on Zoey?

"Gah, you pay me to know stuff. *Pffft*." Her lips made an obscene noise and she shrugged before her expression grew more somber. "I just wish you'd take care of yourself the way you do other people."

Mercer forced a smile and thought about Zoey. He *did* want to see her again—*his* way.

***

Cheyenne Regional Medical Center, West
Noon

Zoey combed Kaity's wet hair to keep it from tangling. She'd washed it for her and bought her new pajamas to wear. She wanted to distance Kaity from what happened to her, but only time and the patience of love would help her friend get through the long journey toward any semblance of recovery.

It broke her heart to see her friend in the throes of her torment.

Zoey had slept on a cot in her hospital room. When she couldn't sleep, she watched over her friend and caught her crying. Or Kaity would wake in the middle of the night, screaming. The nurses would sedate her, but her dearest friend needed someone with a lot of staying power to take care of her.

"I want you to stay with me until you're ready," Zoey said. "I'm not just talking about you getting back on your feet, physically. It's not easy living alone, but after what happened, I want to be there for you. We're family."

"I don't want to be a burden."

"You won't be. After what happened, I could use the company. I was so scared. I thought I'd never see you again." She hugged Kaity and kissed her cheek. "You'd be doing it for me, if that's okay."

"Oh, yeah. Sure. Thank you." Her friend tried to smile, but her swollen lip hurt. "Hey, whatever happened to that nice cop, the one who saved my life and told me about you searching for me? What he said made me think he knew you well, like you were...friends."

Zoey's eyes misted, but she shrugged off the emotion she still felt for Mr. January. She knew the man had many secrets, the first being his identity. Not even Detective Cruz could break through his sealed records and the cop had raised the hackles of the Feds for merely querying his fingerprints. It didn't feel right to keep what she knew about Mr. January from Kaity, but for *his* sake, it felt like the right thing to do.

"I talked to a lot of cops trying to search for you. Maybe he wanted you to feel safe and he used my name. You know, something familiar to help you—"

Before she could finish, Zoey's phone rang. Detective Estefan Cruz's name appeared on the display and she freaked.

What now? I definitely don't need this.

"I have to take it. I'll be right back."

She stepped into the hallway and headed for an empty waiting room down the corridor.

"Detective Cruz. I was going to call you when I got back to Denver. I'm still in Wyoming, at the hospital with my friend."

"Yes, I heard. Cheyenne PD contacted me after you suggested they make the call. They told me you found your friend, Kaity Boyer. In Wyoming?"

Zoey did ask that Cruz be notified. She didn't want the three women who died in the warehouse fire to not find justice. With the cases connected, the police could coordinate their investigations to link the murders and abductions to the trafficking ring Mr. January and his team had found.

"I still can't believe it. Kaity would've died if—" Zoey couldn't finish. With her eyes shut tight, she held the cell phone to her ear and thought of the many ways her search for Kaity could've ended if she hadn't crossed paths with Mr. January.

Zoey plopped down on a waiting room sofa and sighed while she listened to the detective. The guy didn't know when to quit. He reminded her...*of her*.

"CPD was sketchy on the details," he said. "How exactly did you find her?"

"That wasn't me. I actually don't know how it happened. You'll have to ask the Cheyenne police. It looked like their SWAT team brought Kaity to the hospital. There were other victims, too. The police must've gotten a tip."

"But how did you know to be in Wyoming? And where were you staying when you heard?"

"Those are all...very good questions. You must be good at your job."

"Did your mystery man have anything to do with this?"

"I have no idea. Like you told me before, the guy has no name. If you couldn't find out anything about him, how do you expect a civilian to get the jump on you? What did the Feds tell you? They talked to you about him, right?"

"I can't say."

"I guess that makes two of us." Zoey needed a diversion to change the subject from Mr. January. "Were you able to link the murders of those three women in the burned warehouse to the trafficking ring they discovered in Wyoming? I heard the police found gasoline doused over the hostages. One of the bastards was about to torch the place. It's a good thing the police stopped him in time."

"I'm working with the Cheyenne authorities. We're sorting things out, but it'll take time. If I have any questions, I'll call you."

"I'm not sure what I can contribute, detective, but if it makes you feel good, knock yourself out. I'll give it my best shot."

"Yeah, you do that."

When she ended the call, a shadow eclipsed the doorway and she looked up to see Mr. January staring at her. Zoey forgot to breathe. She wished she had a button to stop time, just to feast her eyes on him and have time for second helpings. He wore faded jeans, a blue chambray shirt unbuttoned to show his broad chest, and a leather jacket and boots, but it hadn't been difficult to imagine him without a stitch on. If she could choose a waking dream, he would be it, especially if he had ice cream with him and two spoons. With his intense eyes fixed on her, she forced herself to breathe again.

Zoey couldn't help it. She grinned until her cheeks hurt.

"Your conversation with the detective would've gone a lot smoother if you told him about me." He smiled. "But I appreciate your discretion."

"I didn't think I'd see you again."

"I wasn't sure about that myself." He stepped into the waiting room and sat on the sofa next to her, close enough for her to feel the warmth off his body. "But I wanted to thank you."

"Me? For what?"

"For reminding me what real love is...and how good it feels." He touched her cheek to brush back a strand of her hair. "The way you love Kaity, it took guts to risk everything for her. You're an amazing woman and I haven't stopped thinking about that kiss...our kiss."

"Me too."

"I need you to understand, I'm not exactly free," he said. "I've got baggage that hasn't been easy, but you opened my eyes to...how my life could be again. I don't have to accept things the way they are. I can change what matters, if..."

"Are you...married? Are you involved with someone?"

"No, but it's not that simple. My heart isn't mine to give. Not yet. There's something I need to do first."

He took her hand in his and kissed her fingers. "I don't want secrets between us."

"But from what I understand from Detective Cruz, you're a ghost. Your background is 'need to know,' which means that what you do is classified." She snuggled closer to him and touched his chest. "I saw those victims you helped. Whatever you're doing, it's important. I can understand your need for secrecy."

"That can be hard on a relationship. We'd have to take it slow."

"Then I propose we take a very important first step," she said.

"What's that?"

She held out her hand.

"Hi, my name is Zoey Meager."

A slow smile spread across his face when he realized what she wanted from him and he reached for her hand.

"Hi, Zoey. My name is Mercer. Mercer Broderick."

Mercer pulled her into his arms and kissed her with such tenderness that she cried. His lips nuzzled her neck and gave her goose bumps. She crawled onto his lap and ran her fingers through his hair, claiming him as hers.

The words of warning from Charlotte swept through her mind, the waitress who had named him Mr. January, when she said *'Sometimes wild things need to stay untamed, honey. That one's a loner, certified. He has a razor sharp edge to him.'*

Maybe Charlotte had him pegged—as a wildling and a loner with a dangerous edge to his nature. Zoey heard the truth in those words, especially knowing how he unselfishly risked his life for others. What he'd chosen to do with his life meant she had to accept him for the man he'd become—and be willing to lose him and risk her heart for the same reason.

Zoey didn't know if that translated to having a future together, but in that moment, she felt certain of one thing—she wanted more 'nows' with this extraordinary man.

***

Laramie Mountains
Dusk

Mercer knew the day would come when he'd have to let go. He'd put if off because his heart wasn't ready. It would never be ready. Grief kept him living in the past and punishing himself for what had happened. He thought his work would be enough to shove his pain deep, but his missions had become walls to keep anyone from getting too close.

It took a stranger to flail at those walls until they cracked. Zoey had broken through to him—a straightforward woman with a big heart. She made him want more and she opened his eyes to a life he never would have glimpsed without her.

Mercer drove his F-150 truck into the Laramie Mountains as the sun spread its molten fire across the sky. Karl sat in the passenger seat as the truck jostled over ruts, following a winding trail Mercer had a hand in creating, before tragedy had changed him forever. When he reached the spot he came to find, he parked his vehicle near a lookout point and got out.

The view always took his breath.

Mercer had discovered the panoramic cliff with his wife, Keara. He'd proposed to her at dusk, standing on this very spot.

A lush basin of rolling hills had spires of evergreen trees dappling its hillsides. A river cut through the gorge, rippling over rocks, with its rushing water glistening in the waning sunlight. When he closed his eyes, he heard the faint whisper of the water. In the upper elevations, sharp, jagged ridges towered over the valley and jutted into a bank of low clouds, to touch heaven.

His eyes misted and his throat tightened when he thought of what he came to do. He returned to his truck and let Karl out. The dog would usually roam, but today his partner sensed something in him and stayed at his side. On the floorboard was a canvas bag. He pulled out its contents and stared down at it.

"One last time, my love."

In his hands he held a wooden box he had carved. He hadn't touched it in a very long time, but it was never far from his mind. Inside the ornate container were the ashes of his wife, Keara, and the remains of his only child—his four-year old son, Braeden.

Mercer had been on a covert assignment with the CIA when his wife and child were brutally murdered four years ago. The police never found the killer. That's when he realized the brittle nature of justice.

He opened the box and cut into the two plastic bags with his pocket knife as tears trailed down his cheeks. In the dying light, his hands sifted through the silken ashes of his beloved wife and child as he stood on the cliff.

"You still are everything to me. My sun, my moon, and the air I breathe. I don't know how I can do this without you, but in your name, I will try to honor our love."

He broke down as he pictured their sweet faces. On the wind he smelled his wife's skin and his little boy's hair after a bath. He remembered the sheer joy of hearing Braeden giggle and how he'd counted Keara's breaths as she slept next to him after she'd told him he would be a father—when she breathed for two—those memories swelled through him in the evening stillness.

"I thought our time together would last forever, but I was deeply and painfully wrong. Please forgive me for—"

They died alone, without him, in utter fear. Mercer shut his eyes, making his fragile peace with a sin that could never be forgiven.

When the last of the precious dust wafted into the wind and carried down into the valley, the sun vanished on the horizon. He pictured the spirits of his wife and child lifted by the unearthly breath of

God over an eternity until his soul could join them and he'd see them again.

He would not hate in their name. He'd remember their love instead.

After his emotional bloodletting ended, Mercer sat on the ground and put his arm around his dog, running his fingers through the scruff of his neck. When Karl licked a salty tear from his cheek, the dog whimpered in commiseration.

"Yeah, I know," Mercer said. "I love you, too."

Hot Target

Tough Target

An Omega Team Novella – Desiree Holt Amazon Kindle World (2 Novellas with connected storylines)

By Jordan Dane

Redemption for Avery

A Special Forces: Operation Alpha Novella – Susan Stoker Amazon Kindle World

(Crossover with Jordan Dane's new Ryker Townsend – FBI Profiler series)

By Jordan Dane

Coming 2017

***Jordan Dane will be writing for these great
Amazon Kindle Worlds:***

Sable Hunter's Hell, Yeah! (May 2017)

Elle James's Brotherhood Protector (June 2017)

Paige Tyler's Dallas Fire & Rescue (July 2017)

Susan Stoker's Special Forces: Operation Alpha (Fall
2017)

About the Author

Bestselling, critically-acclaimed author Jordan Dane's gritty thrillers are ripped from the headlines with vivid settings, intrigue, and dark humor. Publishers Weekly compared her intense novels to Lisa Jackson, Lisa Gardner, and Tami Hoag, naming her debut novel NO ONE HEARD HER SCREAM as Best Books of 2008. She also pens young-adult novels for Harlequin Teen. Formerly an energy sales manager, she now writes full time. Jordan shares her Texas residence with two lucky rescue dogs.

Connect with Jordan Dane:

Social Media Links:

Website-www.JordanDane.com

Twitter-www.twitter.com/JordanDane

Facebook -www.facebook.com/JordanDaneAuthor

Pinterest–www.pinterest.com/jordandane

Thriller/Crime Fiction Blogs:

The Kill Zone –www.killzoneblog.com

Sign Up for Jordan Dane's Mailing List for Exclusive Content:

http://www.jordandane.com/mailing.php

Bibliography

Avon/HarperCollins Titles:

NO ONE HEARD HER SCREAM–Standalone

NO ONE LEFT TO TELL–No One Series Book 1

NO ONE LIVES FOREVER–No One Series Book 2

EVIL WITHOUT A FACE–Sweet Justice Book 1

THE WRONG SIDE OF DEAD–Sweet Justice Book 2

THE ECHO OF VIOLENCE–Sweet Justice Book 3

RECKONING FOR THE DEAD–Sweet Justice Book 4

**Omega Team Novellas: Desiree Holt's
Amazon Kindle World:**

HOT TARGET (Novella 1 of 2)

TOUGH TARGET (Novella 2 of 2)

IN THE EYES OF THE DEAD (Crossover: Jordan Dane's Ryker Townsend Series)

Special Forces: Operation Alpha – Susan Stoker's Amazon Kindle World:
REDEMPTION FOR AVERY (Crossover: Jordan Dane's Ryker Townsend Series)

Mercer Broderick Series:
MR. JANUARY (Mercer's War Book #1)

Harlequin Teen Young Adult Novels:
IN THE ARMS OF STONE ANGELS
ON A DARK WING
INDIGO AWAKENING–Hunted Series Book 1 of 2
CRYSTAL STORM–Hunted Series Book 2 of 2

YA Anthologies:
NYX IN THE HOUSE OF NIGHT–"The Magic of Being Cherokee" essay: Smart Pop Books

Cosas Finas Publications:
BLOOD SCORE (Gabe Cronan Novel)
THE LAST VICTIM (Ryker Townsend Novel-Book 1)
MR. JANUARY (Mercer's War Book #1)

Cosas Finas Publications: Non-fiction

ONE AUTHOR'S AHA MOMENTS – Author Craft
Book with a Focus on Writing YA

Ryker Townsend FBI Profiler Series: In Order

THE LAST VICTIM (Ryker Townsend Novel-Book 1)

REDEMPTION FOR AVERY (Ryker Townsend
Novella-Book 2)

IN THE EYES OF THE DEAD (Ryker Townsend
Novella-Book 3)